I could recall it well, that conversation, and one word of it now stood out particularly clearly in my mind: an accident, a nasty accident. That great flowerpot, earth-filled, that could kill a man. I eased it slowly towards the corner where the broken rail was. What a weight it was! I looked up and around the square; there were a few people about, but no one was looking in my direction. Why should they? I pushed the pot a little nearer. Should I leave it there and then await my moment?

I leaned forward, holding on ever more tightly to the sash, and just below my balcony was the head of thick hair and the brown sueded shoulders underneath, and my foot came up to the rim of the flowerpot and it kicked, and with the effort and the strain and the attempt not to fall myself, my hand came down too hard on the edge of the sash window, and it gave way, and the great weight came crashing down and I with it. . . .

THE DARKENED ROOM

Books by Anna Clarke
From The Berkley Publishing Group

THE DARKENED ROOM

ANNA CLARKE

B

BERKLEY BOOKS, NEW YORK

This Berkley book contains the complete text
of the original hardcover edition. It has been
completely reset in a typeface designed for
easy reading, and was printed from new film.

THE DARKENED ROOM

A Berkley Book / published by arrangement with
the author

PRINTING HISTORY
John Long Limited edition published 1968
Berkley edition / March 1991

ISBN: 0-425-12622-6

A BERKLEY BOOK ® TM 757,375
Berkley Books are published by The Berkley Publishing Group,
200 Madison Avenue, New York, New York 10016.
The name "BERKLEY" and the "B" logo
are trademarks belonging to Berkley Publishing Corporation.

PRINTED IN THE UNITED STATES OF AMERICA

10 9 8 7 6 5 4 3 2 1

THE DARKENED ROOM

1

It would do.

The carpet was threadbare and the wallpaper was scratched and dirty and the tiny cooker was thickly encrusted with burnt food, but the room was large and airy, had running water and adequate heating, and above all it was a safe refuge. For where could one hope for greater anonymity, where—so long as one paid the rent and created no nuisance—could one live in such total seclusion, an object of complete indifference to all around, than in a third rate lodging house in the heart of London?

The fugitive makes for the security of the crowd. I had climbed the flight of stairs as if I were indeed on the run, and stood impatiently at the door waiting for the limping old caretaker. She would not trouble me; it had cost her much effort to come up from the basement. To take in parcels and receive the rents, that was all she was fit for. No tiresome chatty landlady there. I thanked her and bade her good evening and watched her hobble away.

It would do. Here I could hide. Behind me was a thin partition and a door with a Yale lock and all the comings and goings of the others in the house who were nothing to me nor I to them; and in front of me was a vast sash window, the biggest I had ever seen, reaching from floor to

1

ceiling, and beyond it a little balcony with iron railings, and
beyond that again were the plane trees in the square,
silhouetted against the delicate pinks and greens of the
evening sky. It was near the end of April and it had been a
day of sun and showers. With all my search for a haven, my
flight from the horror that would not die, I had yet thought
to miss the sunsets and the freshness and freedom of my
Cornish home. But this evening was beautiful, magical. If
I could not sit on the terrace and gaze dreamily out to sea,
I could at least put a chair on the balcony and look at the
flowers in the square. And I could put some flowerpots
there myself.

I was exhausted and I was overwrought and if I had had
any sense I would have gone straight to bed, but the sky and
the balcony drew me, and I clicked back the window catch
and pushed at the heavy sash. To my surprise it slid up
easily and I crept underneath, slowly and carefully, making
sure the balcony would bear my weight. I watched the
darkening sunset colours until my whole being seemed
submerged in them and for several minutes I forgot all that
I had been, all that I still was, all that was yet to come. And
then the air struck chill and I bent down and crawled back
under the sash window into the room, and raised my arms
to pull it down.

It would not budge. For ten minutes or more I heaved and
pulled and strained and then I sat on the bed and held my
head in my hands and cried a little in weakness and despair.
And then I shivered, because the breeze was indeed cold,
and I thought of all the long sleepless hours of the night and
it was more than I could bear. The caretaker was useless,
and to ask the police—but I shuddered afresh at the thought
of asking the police.

Who lived in this house? Middle-aged women, alone and
slightly odd? Rowdy students? Dirty, ineffectual bachelors?
There must be someone, surely, who would help, but who
would not be the least bit interested in me. And should any

explanation be required, I had a name, an identity, a reason for being here. I was a historical researcher, taking digs near the British Museum for a few weeks in order to do some reading there for my employer, an eminent scholar who lived in the west country and never came to town. That would be ample for Bloomsbury; with luck I need say nothing.

I opened my door and stood on the landing. It felt strange and rather frightening, not knowing what creatures lived and breathed behind those closed doors, all painted in the same violent shade of blue. There was a loud swell of music and the sound of gunfire from behind the door next to my own. A Western or a thriller, and that might well mean a man in the house. I had heard it as I stood in my room; the wall was very thin, the television set full on.

I hesitated. There was a sound from the landing above, and I started and stepped back hastily into my room. The night air made it cold and unfriendly. I began to scold myself. This was ridiculous. I could not avoid my neighbors for ever. I wanted to become accepted unquestioningly in my stated identity, not to attract attention and arouse suspicion by popping in and out of doors like this. There was a loud crescendo and then silence and then shouts and more gunfire. What sort of people could they be? I composed my features into a deprecating smile, made ready to speak a trifle breathlessly, stepped once more out on to the landing and knocked on their door.

The girl who opened it was so startlingly beautiful that my mask slipped and my carefully prepared phrase fled from my mind. She was very tall—a good five foot ten in flat heeled slippers—and was dressed in an ill-fitting grey suit that was none too clean. Her fair hair was pinned up in an attempt at an Edwardian sweep but it wasn't very successful and there were many loose wisps. But when you saw her face you ceased to think of that. It sounds exaggerated, and even silly in these days of over-painted

tow-haired dolls or dead-white straggle-haired beatniks, to
describe it as angelic, but this was the word that came to my
mind then and remained with me every time I saw her. The
eyes were limpid grey, with natural long dark lashes; the
nose classic, the mouth a sweet and generous pink rosebud,
the complexion faultless. She smiled, and it was as if a saint
in a religious painting had come to life and stepped down
out of the frame.

I explained my errand. She doesn't recoil from me, I told
myself with a little lift of the heart; she looks on me simply
as an unknown woman asking for help; this glorious being
will take me for whatever I like to seem to be.

"Oh dear," she said, "they're a frightful nuisance, these
windows—we never open ours at the bottom. Just a
minute—I'll ask Tom."

A husband, I thought with a sudden cold stab of disap-
pointment, and then I instantly scolded myself: don't be a
fool, Mary; of course she would have a husband, and even
if she did not, what could she be to you? Lie low, lie low,
be careful. That's why you are here. But my heart was
beating fast and my tiredness had fled and my mind was
taking leaps into forbidden heavens as I stood there waiting
to see what kind of man had won this paragon.

Good-natured, seemingly. She spoke a few words and
then the television sound was turned low and a young man
appeared at the door. I noticed only that he was a trifle taller
than she was and that he wore a magnificent mohair
sweater. The work of his angel wife, no doubt, I thought,
and again I felt the sudden chill.

"I'm so sorry to trouble you," I began to prattle, "and I
do hope you don't think I'm going to be pestering you all
the time, but I really don't know what to do, and . . ."

"Oh that's all right," broke in the girl. "Tom doesn't
mind. Do you, darling?"

"Not a bit. It was a rotten programme, anyway."

His voice was less cultured than his wife's and it struck

me that she had married beneath her. He was probably a year or so younger too, and it was obvious even on this first encounter that it was the wife who took the lead.

"I'm Judy Prescott, and this is my husband Tom," she said as I led the way into my room. "We've been wondering all evening who was moving in next door. The last person here was an old man who was going a bit potty and he used to cook the most ghastly smelling things—gosh, it *is* cold, isn't it?"

She stood still and looked around her with unconcealed curiosity. Tom walked over to the window and tugged at it without success. Then Judy and I took one side while he took the other, but still we could not move it at all. Then he asked us to move away again while he had another go, and for several minutes he strained and grunted and swore while we stood helplessly by.

"If only Malcolm were here—he'd think up something," said Judy.

Even in my preoccupied state of mind—a mixture of weariness, guilt, and apprehensive excitement—this struck me as a hardly tactful remark to make to a husband who was going to such trouble to help a complete stranger, but he didn't seem to mind at all, and replied with perfect good humour: "Yes, Malcolm'd probably think of something."

"Couldn't we get him to come and help you, then?" I asked, supposing Malcolm to be some relation of the old caretaker, or perhaps one of the other tenants in the house.

They both smiled at me in a faintly pitying manner and informed me that Malcolm could hardly be expected to come all the way from Hampstead to Bloomsbury just to help shift a stuck window, and in any case he was not usually free on a Saturday evening. Then why drag him in at all, I thought with some irritation, and then my tiredness came out on top of all my other feelings and I longed to be rid of them.

"Please don't trouble any more," I begged. "I'll hang a

rug up for the night and push the bed in the corner behind
the washplace out of the draught and get the fire brigade or
something in the morning."

Judy laughed unexpectedly. It was a rather harsh laugh,
the first jarring note I had remarked in her. "That'll cost you
five pounds," she said. "Tom did it once—last summer
before we got married—locked himself out of the top floor
flat. They had to break it open and made a frightful mess."

"Well, it's my own silly fault and I'll just have to pay for
it," I said, "but don't try any more. I've wasted quite
enough of your time."

I was so tired that I could hardly command my voice and
I prayed that they did not notice how I was shaking. Go, go,
for God's sake go and leave me alone, my mind cried out,
and I could not be sure that I had not said it aloud. It was so
many months since I had spoken to anyone but shopkeepers
or bus conductors that thought and speech had become
confused. I talked to myself, I was sure. But had I spoken
now? It seemed to me that both looked at me curiously. I
hugged my arms around myself and shivered.

"Oh you poor thing, you *are* cold!" exclaimed Judy. "We
can't possibly leave you like this—can we, darling?"

Thank heaven, I thought, I had not said the words aloud.

Tom spoke: "No, of course not. I wonder if one of the
boys is in."

"Or Dr. Strangeways. Do go and see, Tom. And if not,
we can always try the Indians."

Tom Prescott left the room. I sat on the edge of the bed
and held my head in my hands. I was near to tears.

"Please, please," I begged, "don't go troubling all these
people. You can't think how I hate being so tiresome. So
stupid, so stupid."

I could say no more.

"I shouldn't worry about that," said Judy cheerfully. She
was prowling about the room now, being very obviously
tactful and giving me a chance to recover. "We're a very

friendly sort of house here—I'm sure you'll like it. Dennis and Harry are students and they've got the flat underneath, and the Indians are all at the top and they don't disturb you much, and Dr. Strangeways—he lectures at the university—he's above this, and so is Liz. She's an art student and I expect you'll like her."

Why, I thought, why shall I like her? Could this chattering commonplace girl with the incredibly beautiful face have guessed already at my weakness? Impossible. I was overtired, unused to human contact, imagining things. I must make some effort to take a grip on myself and play my part or I should arouse suspicion at once.

"I expect I'll be seeing them some time," I said with a fair attempt at the manner of a poised and not very interested woman of the world, "but I'm going to be pretty busy while I'm here. I've got a lot of work to do at the British Museum and shan't have much time for anything else."

"The Museum? Why, Dr. Strangeways is working there now!"

She sounded delighted, and I had a sudden vision of her in twenty years' time as a plump, loquacious matron, joyfully exclaiming "The world's a small place!" on hearing of some particularly banal item of coincidence. As to one of my fellow lodgers frequenting the British Museum, this was so likely a contingency in this university area that I had been prepared for it and was not unduly dismayed. My work was no secret; so long as I kept to myself the name of the scholar for whom I was acting I had nothing to fear.

"Really?" I said coolly, and had the satisfaction of seeing her look a little disconcerted. "No doubt quite a number of the people around here are doing likewise."

"Yes, I suppose so. He's a bit mysterious though," she said, brightening up again, "and Malcolm says he's either running a teenage dope racket or has run away from his wife."

Malcolm again. This wretched Malcolm. Judy Prescott's very accent seemed to take on another personality when she mentioned him and there came a little extra animation into her face and she giggled like a schoolgirl referring to her favourite pop-singer. It was on the tip of my tongue to question her about Malcolm, but this was so obviously just what she wanted me to do that I restrained myself.

"If you'll excuse me," I said, "at least I can be getting on with making up my bed."

She insisted on helping me. She tucked in the sheets crookedly and let the blankets lie in ridges and I bit back my annoyance and thanked her, reflecting that I should have to re-make it after she had gone.

"Is there anything else I can do?" she asked.

I was saved from having to reply by her husband's return. He brought with him a short, dark, middle-aged man with heavy rimmed glasses, who gave one cursory glance at me and then walked purposefully over to the window. Tom Prescott followed him—it seemed to me that he was the sort of young man who would always be following just behind someone or other—and they stood side by side at the great window and gripped the top of the lower sash.

"Now—both at once," said the newcomer, whom I guessed to be Dr. Strangeways. The window came down at an alarming speed and with a crash that shook the house. The two men staggered as if their opponents in a tug-of-war had suddenly given way, and nearly lost their balance.

"Hooray!" cried Judy and clapped her hands.

I came forward to thank them.

" 'fraid the sash-cord's gone," said Tom.

"It doesn't matter," I said. "I'll get it mended later."

"You'd better be careful with that window," said the short dark man abruptly. "Could be dangerous."

I thanked him again and said I would be very careful and then it seemed to me that they all ought to go and leave me to get to bed in peace, but they all three stood looking frowningly at the window, as if it were some sort of monster that could move of its own accord, and Judy said: "It's funny they ever made them that size," and then there was a rush of footsteps on the stairs and two young men came hurrying into the room.

"What on earth's going on?"

"Thought the house was coming down!"

Judy took it upon herself to explain and the boys proceeded to stare at the window too. I stood behind them, speechless with frustration, aching for them to go, momentarily wishing myself back in the solitary siege of my own dear home. I had lived so many months away from my fellows that I had forgotten how tiresome ordinary human beings could be. The window continued to fascinate them all. The short man and the boys were surveying it in a disapproving way, while Tom was examining the broken sash-cord with the infuriating slow deliberation of the self-styled handyman. I knew exactly what was coming next. It was unrolling itself like a well-worn gramophone record, and old film reel. "Do you know, I believe I can fix that window," he said.

"I shouldn't mess about with it if I were you," said the short dark man, and then he left the room with as little ceremony as he had entered it, and without looking at me or saying goodnight. A fugitive like myself? Or just extremely shy? At any rate he had broken the spell because the two boys, who were both thin and fair haired and rather alike, seemed suddenly to recollect themselves and they looked at me in some embarrassment and apologised for intruding and disappeared too.

The Prescotts remained.

"Have you had any supper?" asked Judy. "Can I get you an egg or something?"

"I had a good meal on the train," I lied, "and really all I want is to get to bed."

"Oh yes. It's frightfully exhausting, moving." She gave

me a melting glance of sympathy and I began to hope that I might have my room to myself before many more minutes were over. "Tom. Tom darling," she went on, "you can't do any more tonight. We must leave Miss—Mrs. . . ."

"Miss Wentworth." It cost me a great effort to say it, but it had to be done sooner or later.

"—leave Miss Wentworth in peace. Can't you see she's worn out?"

"Oh well." Tom abandoned the window reluctantly. "I'll have a go at it tomorrow though, if you like."

It was too cruel to refuse him. I cannot snub people who are trying to help. It is one of my many weaknesses. "Not too early, please," was my one stipulation.

They moved to the door at last, and I was already drawing in my breath for the big sigh of relief, when they stopped yet again:

"Oh by the way, what Sunday papers do you take?"

It was Tom who spoke. I goggled at him. I was dazed with fatigue and wondered if I had heard aright. Judy explained:

"Tom always goes out and buys the papers. He's always up first and likes a bit of air first thing. We have the *Express* and the *Sunday Mirror* and Dennis and Harry have the *News of the World* and the *Observer* and Dr. Strangeways has the *Observer* and the *Sunday Times* and Liz—what does Liz have, darling?"

In happier days I might have been interested in this summary readership survey, but just now it was the last straw. "I don't want any," I said weakly.

When at last I shut the door behind them and let the Yale lock click into place I felt as whacked as if I had just been on a cross country run and had not slept for a month. I did not even tidy the bed, but unpacked the bare essentials, swallowed two sleeping pills with a cup of black Nescafé, and crept between the sheets. I lay long in a semi-stupor, motionless, without rational sequence of thought. Dream-like figures came and went, all with the faces of the strangers who had surrounded me in my room. Sometimes they were threatening, sometimes they were friendly; always they were oppressive, disturbing my peace and my solitude, and dominating them all, lit up by an ethereal glow and smiling at me with the most delicious tilt of those rosebud lips, was the wonderful face of Judy Prescott.

2

When the blessed gift of sleep had spent itself and the struggle against daylight and returning consciousness had finally proved in vain, I found to my surprise that a little flicker of hopeful anticipation was mingled with the paralysing despair that ushered in my every new day. It puzzled me until it resolved itself into the face of Judy Prescott, and the events of the previous evening sorted themselves out in my mind. This beautiful creature was no dream vision, but was a living girl, and she was at this very moment breathing and sleeping or moving and speaking only a few yards away from me. The thought excited me so much that for the first time in many months I rose quickly from my bed, pulled aside the window curtains and looked with interest on the world outside.

The sun shone on the green of the grass and the gold of the daffodils, on the garish red of a telephone booth and on the metallic blue and grey of the cars parked at the side of the square. A milk float rattled by; a couple of Negro students in college scarves crossed the road talking earnestly. A mongrel dog sniffed at the lamp-post, and a young man came out to throw buckets of soapy water over his car. The heart of London on a Sunday morning; a still centre of the world. I half-closed my eyes, and the view stood out in splashes of colour like a child's painting. I told myself that

13

I was on the run, driven from my home by the cruel gossip that was never allowed to die down, by my own memories of horror that never left me. I tried to remember that sunlight and people and life were my enemies, that I must hide in my room like a fox in its hole and shun all human contact. But all I could see was a bright and peaceful morning, innocent, harmless, unthreatening people, and all of it somehow linked up in my heart and mind with the radiance that was Judy Prescott's face.

There was a knock at the door. I did not even start, but put my dressing-gown around me and went to open it. She was even more lovely in old black jeans and a blue sweater than she had been in her shabby suit. She had not yet pinned up her hair and it hung around her face in a golden mist, like a pre-Raphaelite picture. One caught one's breath just to look at her, and inevitably the thought came that she ought to be enchanting millions on small or large screen, or gracing some big social gathering, clad in model dresses that would be worthy of her, instead of slopping around in a Bloomsbury lodging house, married to a very ordinary young man and apparently quite content with it.

But was she in fact content? The girl fascinated me, quite apart from her beauty. What was she really like? What lay underneath that astonishing exterior? At least, I thought, she was not frightened of me—not yet. I had made no bad impression, had aroused sympathetic interest, not malicious curiosity. That much was apparent from her words, for in her low voice, diffident and yet persistent, she was apologising for intruding. "You must think we're awful, pestering you like this. I know people like to be left in peace, but we were so worried about you, Tom and I. You looked so tired last night and it's awful moving in and not having anything you need, and—well, we didn't see how you *could* have any breakfast with you really, and I've bought far too much bacon as usual and it won't keep, and we'd love it if you'd come and have some—or I could bring it to you in here if you'd rather be alone. I *do* hope you don't think we're being an awful nuisance," she finished more fluently.

Bacon! I became aware that for the first time in many months I was genuinely hungry. The very idea of the black coffee and apples and biscuits on which I had intended to live till the Monday morning sickened me. Bacon! It was irresistible. Of course she would be a rotten cook, but to receive it at those hands . . . !

I smirked at her. "That's most thoughtful and charming of you. I'd very much like to come."

Perhaps my lips had grown so unused to smiling that it looked more like a grimace; perhaps I had been guilty of my great failing of sounding affected and over-eager—after all, it is not for nothing that I am the daughter of one of the best-known theatrical partnerships of their generation—but my reaction seemed to disturb her, and I had the impression that she recoiled slightly.

"It'll be about ten minutes then, if that's all right," she said. "We're not—we're not terribly posh, you know."

"It's awfully kind of you, really," I said, thinking that the best way to put her at her ease would be to imitate her own manner of speech. Whatever her true nature might be she was surely not subtle; she would not see my mockery.

"About ten minutes then," she said again.

I had learned from last night that both she and her husband were of the breed that finds it extremely difficult to get itself out of a room. I thanked her again and walked determinedly over to my little washing alcove. She went.

For an English housewife to spoil a conventional English breakfast is quite a feat, but Judy Prescott came near to achieving it. In all fairness, however, I had to admit that she seemed nervous and a little in awe of me, and her renewed apologies for their humble way of living told me plainly enough in what social class they had placed me. We ate underdone bacon and burnt toast and I found it difficult to believe that even the most worshipping of husbands would put up with this day after day without any complaint. But today at any rate Tom had the sense to say nothing, and I was agreeably surprised at this and looked at him with some interest.

A totally commonplace young man. A not unpleasant face, but the snub nose and the protruding ears and the accent that grated a little spoke only too clearly of the background from which he had sprung. Messing about with tools and watching television Westerns—that would be just about his measure. And his angel wife liked knitting and trying a new hairdo. And they both liked being on chatty terms with their neighbours. A pattern that might be repeated a hundred times in any suburban street. And yet there was something rather unusual about them, something rather helpless and vulnerable. They did not seem to me to have quite their fair share of that brashness and self-confidence that is such a common characteristic among the youth of today. They seemed to be on the lookout for other people's opinions to adopt, other people's advice to follow. This unknown Malcolm, for instance, whom I was already beginning to dislike, was mentioned as soon as we sat down to the meal. I had remarked on the Picasso reproduction that hung over the mantelpiece and which was so out of keeping with the characterless furniture of the room.

"Oh, Malcolm gave us that," said Judy, "and the Swedish glasses. Aren't they nice? When we get our house we're going to have it all in that style."

"You're going to buy a house, then?"

They both began to speak at once, Judy always slightly in the lead. Yes, they were saving up for the deposit, half their pay every month went straight into the bank. Tom worked for the Greater London Council and was studying for the professional exams and Judy was a secretary in a university institute. They were both of them interested in their salaries, the people they worked for, and the work itself, in that order. I mentally drafted out my own story as I listened.

They would be asking questions soon and it was as well to be prepared.

"I've been living in Cornwall, looking after an elderly relative," I said when my turn came. This was not too far from the truth, and easy enough to embellish if necessary. I knew too little of any other part of the country safely to sustain a fiction that I had come from anywhere else. "After she died I thought I'd like a change," I went on, "and I've got this job copying from documents at the British Museum for an author, so I shall stay here until I've finished and then see if I can't find something else and perhaps look around for a flat. But I'm not going to overwork—I'm rather tired and want to take things quietly for a bit."

"That's just what I said," exclaimed Judy triumphantly. "I said to Tom, she's had a bad time, you can see it in her eyes, and she needs a rest."

"And I said you were country—Devon or Cornwall probably," added Tom, "so we're both right."

I shivered inwardly at the thought that they had already been discussing me, but I managed to laugh it away. "Good heavens, do I look like the pages of *Country Life* or talk like the Archers! I really don't know whether to be insulted or flattered!"

They both laughed too, and there was a happy little feeling of good fellowship between the three of us which drove away my apprehension and I thought how easy it was, among strangers of goodwill who knew nothing of my story, to play a part and gain their trust.

"We're ever so glad you've come so that we've got someone nice next door," said Judy, "and I hope you won't go away just yet. Actually most of the people in the house at the moment are all right, but you never know who's coming."

"And how do you know I'm going to be a good neighbour?" I asked, still smiling. It was a measure of my new-found confidence that I dared to ask the question.

"Well, because—well you *look* all right. I mean, anyone can see that you're not going to have all-night parties or sweep your rubbish out on the landing."

"I see," I said as lightheartedly as before. "Respectable middle-aged ladies are presumably all right. But it doesn't always follow, you know. Some very undesirable characters have appeared on the surface to be harmless middle-aged ladies."

You're crazy, I told myself even as I spoke; crazy. Don't push your luck too far. But they merely laughed again and then Tom said: "Oh yes, of course the murderer is always the least likely person—but that's in books, not in real life."

"Do you like detective stories?" I asked, and the conversation changed to reading matter, and before we had managed more than a couple of sentences, up popped Malcolm again. Apparently he guided their reading as well as their artistic taste. His opinions were quoted at length and there came into the eyes of the young couple the devout look that I had noticed the previous evening when his name was mentioned. It was time, I thought, if I were to live here on friendly terms with these two, that I got this Malcolm business straight. That they had accepted me completely I now had no doubt, but that their lives were so dominated by another, by one who might look on me with very different eyes, this caused me great unease.

"He sounds an interesting person, your friend," I remarked. "Is he a journalist by profession?"

This produced a flood, as I had expected it would. No, Malcolm wasn't exactly a journalist, although he did quite a bit of writing and had had a book of poems published. He also did some illustrating—book jackets mostly. And he was a marvellous violin player and played in a string quartet. No, not exactly one of the well-known ones; he didn't actually perform in concerts; it was more a little group of friends, but they knew one of them was a barrister and another was an author—Malcolm knew all *sorts* of people. No, they didn't know much about music themselves and couldn't understand it really, but it was marvellous all the same. And he'd got a super flat in Hampstead—or rather it was a sort of studio built out from a big house and he'd decorated it all himself and it looked super. Or rather he had not done the actual painting—Tom had done all that—but he'd designed it all, and a lot of the furniture too. He was a marvellous designer and he knew an awful lot about clothes and fashion too and was always going on at Judy to dress better, but she didn't know why, she supposed it was because her parents had been rather old-fashioned and she'd been brought up in a small country town and she'd never really got very interested in clothes or learned how to make the best of herself. But she knew Malcolm was right and she ought to try, and when they'd reached the five hundred mark in their savings at the end of this month she was going to treat herself to some new things and Malcolm had promised to come along and help her choose them, because Tom was no good at clothes either, was he, darling?— although he was always going on about how she ought to dress better too.

"Well, honestly, Miss Wentworth, don't you think Judy is worth taking trouble over?" He looked at her with such a sudden blaze of proud possession that my heart turned over and I felt apprehensive again, though this time it was not entirely for myself.

"Indeed she is," I said, "and I shall look forward to seeing the result of all the expert advice." I spoke as lightly as I could, but the unease continued. This was an odd situation, surely, and not necessarily a very happy one, where best friend was privileged to step in front of husband and choose clothes for beautiful wife. Of course Malcolm might well be a homosexual and his interest in Judy a mere cover-up for his interest in the husband. That would be very convenient for me, I thought wryly, but looking at Tom it did not seem very likely.

"Where did you meet?" I asked.

"Oh we had digs in the same house in Hampstead," was Tom's ready reply. "Liz too. There were a lot of art students."

I noticed then that Judy was pursing her lips in silent disapproval.

"I never had anything to do with them," said Tom defiantly, and I had the impression that this conversation had taken place many times before. "Liz is different. You'll see when you meet her."

"She's a Lesbian," said Judy suddenly and then glanced at me in a furtive manner as if to see how I had taken it. I looked at her without expression and she flushed slightly. "Anyway, Tom doesn't go to any wild parties now," she went on, looking away, "and neither does Malcolm. I think he's a bit prudish at heart—like me." She gave her rather harsh little laugh.

Breakfast was over and I stood up to go. I had survived the ordeal well but for the time being I had had enough. "I have to meet some friends this morning," I lied, and thanked them again.

They looked disappointed, though I could hardly believe they really wanted me to stay longer, and then Judy said:

"Malcolm's coming in to coffee this evening—are you free? He'd love to meet you, I'm sure. You're much more his type—more intellectual, I mean."

I declined firmly and escaped to my own room. It had been a strain indeed. I was shaking with nerves, obsessionally going over the conversation again and again in my head to reassure myself that I had not given myself away. That trivial chat about being a good neighbour, that had done me good I was sure. I sat down in the dirty chintz-covered armchair and looked out of the window. The colours and shapes of the bright morning soothed me and brought me courage. So far I had done well; it would become easier by and by, but meeting Malcolm was going to be a severe test of nerves. Not only did I guess him to be a far shrewder and more critical observer than the young couple themselves, but I was convinced that he in his turn was going to be informed that I was longing to meet him, an "intellectual," one of a similar kind. A bad way to start a relationship at the best of times. Meeting Malcolm would be full of the usual dangers, and more; I must try out my strength first; I must put it off as long as I possibly could.

— 3 —

I avoided it for two weeks, while I consolidated my position with the rest of the house. Tom succeeded in mending my window and rigged up a sort of Heath Robinson contraption by which I could raise and lower the heavy sash. It was quite an ingenious gadget and I was duly appreciative. Naturally it was not his own idea but that of Malcolm, to whom he had put the problem. I bought some little plants and some big flowerpots. Dennis and Harry carried them upstairs for me and placed them on my balcony. I was surprised how much pleasure I derived from making my little garden—I who had been mistress of acres of beautiful coastland—and I was surprised, too, at my interest in improving my shabby room.

I wandered around Bloomsbury and the West End visiting shops, restaurants, and cinemas, safe and unnoticed among the crowds, just another person lengthening the queue, just one more customer at the counter. It gave me great confidence to walk abroad in the full assurance that no one would know me. Even in the Manuscript Room of the Museum, where I worked for several hours every day, I did not lose this blessed sense of relief, and so far from trying to creep in unnoticed I began to feel gratified when the girl at the desk smiled a welcome.

Often I sat at my great window, looking out on the little world of the square, a world that I could destroy or create at will simply by lowering or raising my eyelids. It had somehow become bound up in my mind with Judy's beauty, and together they formed my link with reality, my lifeline, my hope for a future. I was like someone coming slowly back to awareness after a long, long sleep. My life revolved around little daily satisfactions, plans and activities. It was clear and bright and limited, like the view from the window, and all beyond the framework was invisible.

I saw with the eye of convalescence. I realised this myself, but I did not know that others had noticed it until one evening when Liz knocked at my door and asked to borrow some milk. I felt sure it was simply an excuse to visit me, and sure enough, after I had handed her the carton she began to roam about the room, finally coming to a halt in front of the window. She was a conventional beat type, a caricature of an art student, dark and dirty and bedraggled, everything that was repulsive to me. I did not want to know her, but feared to give offence.

"I'd like to paint that," she said abruptly. "Bit corny, though."

"View from my window? It's often been done, hasn't it?" I said casually.

"Oh Lord, yes. I meant I'd like it as someone lying there sick, who had no other view of the world, would see it. Not as a bit cut out of a larger scene by a window frame but as if there were nothing beyond. D'you know what I mean?" She spoke arrogantly, jerking her head back and pushing aside her lanky hair. "I should think you'd know," she went on. "You've been ill yourself, haven't you, and look at it that sort of way."

I stepped forward so that she could not see from my face how disturbed I was by her remarks. The wretched girl was perceptive enough and she had badly shaken me.

"Yes, I do see what you mean," I said as calmly as I

could. "Actually, I've been nursing someone through a long illness and have been very close to this narrowing of vision that you mention. I was thinking about it when you came in as a matter of fact."

"Oh. Yes, I expect you'd be a good nurse. You'd be practical and wouldn't get too soft-hearted."

Damn the girl! How could she keep scoring bulls'-eyes like this? She was doing her best, on this our second meeting, to force me into an intimate conversation, exploiting to the full her natural lack of courtesy and restraint. If I was not very careful she would be strongly hinting that she had recognised me as one of her own kind and would be making advances to me. This was the very last thing that I wanted to happen and I had to prevent it quick.

"No, that's not me," I said brightly, "though true of the best nurses, no doubt. I'm sorry I can't suggest that you come here and paint, but having only this one room—but you have a similar view upstairs, surely? Have you done it at all?"

"Yes, but it's the wrong angle."

"What about the back of the house? There's a rather fascinating arrangement of chimneys."

"Oh I tried that once. Dr. Strangeways let me in when he was away. It wasn't too bad but I didn't like the sky."

I led her on. The danger was averted. She was uncomfortably shrewd and she might well have sensed my interest in other women, but she was also very young and very self-centred and the opportunity to talk about her work was irresistible. I was well on the way to gaining the ascendancy and establishing a more manageable relationship by the time she went. But I resolved to study her habits and to avoid being alone with her if I possibly could, and if necessary to seek shelter with the boys downstairs, with whom I was more at ease than with anyone else in the house. They were nice, cheerful, casual lads, noisy, untidy, with an endless succession of girl friends turning up at all hours, which greatly interested Judy, although she always referred to it in a disapproving manner.

The days passed quietly away, with many little alarms and anxieties and with some moments of downright apprehension and fear, but on the whole with far greater peace of mind and equanimity than I had ever dreamed of during those months of solitude, of hostile faces in the village, frigid politeness in the shops, a whispering when I came in and a great burst of conversation after I had gone—those months when the melancholy whining of the gulls and the crashing of the waves were the friendliest sounds I heard.

I felt no homesickness; the view of the square was refreshment enough, and every morning the familiar pain of waking was eased by the knowledge that some time in the course of the day I should feel that little quickening of excitement, that little stirring of life that came to me whenever I chanced to look upon the wonder of Judy's face.

I was standing on my balcony inspecting the seedlings in the pots on the afternoon of the second Friday after my arrival when I was startled by a loud and peremptory whistle from below. I looked down and there was Judy, just coming back from work. She had on the old grey suit, but it had been cleaned and pressed, and she must have been to the hairdresser in her lunch hour because the fair strands were sculptured and sprayed into rigid curves and there was not a wisp to be seen. I didn't like it. It looked out of place and absurd, as if somebody had put a stiff permanent wave on the Mona Lisa.

"Oh—hullo," I said, straightening up and looking over the railing. I didn't like this business of conversing from balconies either, nor the loud whistle, which was on a par with the occasional sudden harsh laugh. I think she sensed this—she was in some respects very sensitive to other people's feelings—for she said nothing and merely opened her mouth wide, pointed with an exaggerated gesture first to herself, and then to me. I took this to mean that she wanted to come and talk to me, and I nodded and stepped back into my room.

"I'm sorry I whistled," she said at once. "It's not very polite. I do that sometimes—I don't know why. D'you ever find yourself saying something you don't mean at all? Even telling a lie sometimes?" She threw down her handbag and sprawled over my bed. "I mean sometimes they're talking about a book and you know perfectly well you've never read it and no one will care if you have or not and yet when someone asks you, you say you think you have but can't quite remember and then someone says something about it in more detail and you pretend to remember and say 'Oh yes of course.' Why do I do that? It's so silly, isn't it?"

"None of us likes to admit ignorance," I said sententiously.

"Perhaps that's it. But I'm not vain, am I? I don't feel as if I am. I know I'm good-looking—I mean I can't help it, because they used to make an awful fuss of me when I was young and Mum and Dad were always being asked to have me photographed, and people do look at me rather a lot. But I don't really care very much what I look like. Honestly."

That, I thought, sighing to myself, was probably only too true. And yet it was not entirely unspoilt, unself-conscious simplicity. She was naive and yet she was not innocent. It puzzled and tantalised me. But I would have to be very careful, or I would be manoeuvred into the position of a sort of female Malcolm, to be constantly quoted in conversation, held up as a yardstick, brought to people's attention. It might be already too late; I might have already gone further than was safe. I should have kept away from all human contact, but Judy's beauty had drawn me in and there was no turning back. It could bring me only to disaster. It would happen all over again. For a moment I was paralysed by the horror of recollection, and then I looked at Judy's face in the

hope of dispelling it and found therein compensation for all
my fears.

"My dear child," I said in a kindly maternal way, "you
are so lovely that you have every right to be vain. But from
the very little I know of you I don't think you are."

"Don't you? Oh, I'm so glad. I'm glad you think so. It's
difficult sometimes, you know . . ." She paused. Difficult, looking like that, I mentally finished the sentence for
her, but aloud I said:

"Would you like some tea? I'm going to make some in a
moment."

"No thanks. I only came to ask if you'd like to come
tomorrow evening—we're having a bit of a party. A girl
from my office and a friend of Tom's. And the boys are
coming up and Liz said she'd look in. It's my birthday but
it's nothing special at all but I do hope you can come." She
finished in a breathless rush and looked at me most
appealingly.

I had absolutely no alternative but to accept.

"Good-ee," she said like a small child, and then at the
door she turned back: "Malcolm's promised to come too.
I'm *dying* for you two to meet."

So it had to be, and the trace of slyness that I detected in
her smile before she shut the door disturbed me more than
ever. I began to fancy things and the view from my window
no longer held the power to soothe. Did she suspect me?
Had Liz been talking? Was I to be deliberately exposed to
the all-seeing eye of Malcolm, to be forced to give myself
away? Once again my thoughts slid over the edge of the
abyss, and for a crazy moment I convinced myself that this
unknown Malcolm was one and the same person as the only
witness, the only creature in the world besides myself who
really knew. The man who had been with us—Estelle's boy
friend. The man who had caused me to be brought to trial.
Like Malcolm, a writer of sorts; burying himself in Cornwall
to work on his novel and to hang around Estelle. Staying on

after my acquittal to watch and torment me, making sure it was never forgotten, that the village memory would always remain fresh, that the waves of suspicion would rear up again and yet again. Had he followed me to London, traced me to my present hiding place, ingratiated himself with my neighbours?

For a moment the madness held me in its grip and the impulse to pack up and flee was so violent that I had actually pulled open a couple of drawers and thrown some things out on the bed before I realised what I was doing.

Common sense returned. Malcolm had a background, a past year's history, well known to Tom and Judy. It was absolutely impossible that he had been beatnicking around in Cornwall a year ago and on and off ever since. I was building up an absurd and completely unfounded fear of him and it was high time that I met him for myself and obtained the reassurance of seeing him to be the cheap, self-centred poseur and charlatan that he undoubtedly was. A failed artist; a third-rate writer battening on the ignorance of a good-natured and unselfish young couple. Contempt-ible but not necessarily evil. And I must be polite, non-critical, dull and very, very careful.

I arrived late at the party, seeking safety in numbers. I handed over the box of luxury chocolates I had brought for Judy and was rewarded with a delicious upward turn of the sweet lips. It had cost me great self-restraint to limit myself to this conventional offering, when my fancy was playing with rare cameos and long sapphire ear-rings and other such adornments for Judy's beauty, but it was far too risky to bring anything but the most impersonal of offerings. I was grateful for other reasons, too, when Judy proudly showed me the little diamanté brooch that was Tom's present. It did not suit her at all; but then neither did the little-girl pink shift dress and the sophisticated hairdo that was already sadly deteriorating. There were about half a dozen young people in the room, and I guessed from the fact that I was allowed to go and talk to the boys from downstairs that

Malcolm was not yet among them. Tom poured out over-large measures of spirits, as people of his class so often do—showing off their generosity by forcing unwanted drinks upon their guests—while Judy handed round savouries.

"I was lazy and extravagant and got them all at Fort-nums," she whispered to me.

"Very sensible," I replied, and was glad to be spared her efforts at party cooking, though I could sense a kind of expectancy in her manner that took from me much of my small store of self-confidence.

Liz sidled up to me. "I like your dress," she said, and managed to make the commonplace compliment sound impudent. "I do wish I could afford to buy clothes."

"I'm glad you like it," I said.

She continued to stare and I bore the scrutiny as well as I could, hoping that I had done right in wearing something good but obviously far from new. It belonged to my aunt whom I nursed till her death, I told myself while I stood listening to the youngsters chatting about op art and how best to cook spaghetti; and so did the necklace. She had always promised them to me. Mentally I developed the character of this mythical aunt. Think yourself into the part. I remembered vividly from my childhood how the whole character of the household would change according to the role my mother was playing at the time.

Tom filled my glass. "Malcolm's late," he said, "but he shouldn't be long now." He nodded reassuringly and moved on.

Once again I took refuge with Dennis and Harry. I must not panic; I must keep my head and live in my role; I must start an enthralling conversation with the boys and not even notice Malcolm's arrival. But Judy called me away to admire her flowers.

"Sue brought the irises and Dennis the tulips, and Liz brought the freesias—they're a bit off but she hasn't much money and it's nice of her to buy anything—and Bernard brought the narcissus, and I only hope Malcolm doesn't bring flowers too because I've used up all my vases."

I admired the gifts and the cards on the mantelpiece and picked up a highly coloured cookbook that someone had sent her.

"What luscious pictures," I said. "May I look at it?"

"Oh yes—there're some fabulous Yugoslav recipes. I thought I'd try them."

She moved away. I held tight to the book and pretended to be deeply absorbed in it. With luck it would carry me through Malcolm's arrival and give me a chance to absorb the shock. I stared unseeing at a full-page colour plate of a chocolate gateau, concentrating all my mind and my strength on facing the ordeal to come, hardly conscious of the cheerful noise that was going on around me. And then there was a knock at the door and the talking died away and I had the impression of tension among others in the room besides myself.

He made his entry like a prima donna at the beginning of the first act, whose voice soars above the chattering chorus and who then pauses to hold both audience and stage in hushed and taut expectancy.

My first feeling was one of complete surprise. Subconsciously I had been building up his portrait: shortish, dark, unprepossessing, with heavy spectacles and a straggly beard. All the usual paraphernalia of artistic temperament. As odious in appearance as in character, and speaking, in spite of strenuous efforts to hide it, with an accent that revealed his lower middle class origins. A small trader's son from Oldham or Bradford perhaps.

I positively blinked. Here was a Nordic hero, a Greek god—whatever hackneyed generic term is employed to depict outstanding male beauty. He was tall, very slender, straight, and elegant; hair thick and brown and only slightly longer than my conventional judgement approved, eyes startlingly blue. And he was dressed in sober grey, in a suit that must have cost all of sixty guineas, and his tie was to match and was faultless.

All this I saw before I noticed that he came awkwardly, sideways, into the room, arms behind him in an attempt to conceal what they held. Judy had opened the door to him. From where I stood by the window I had a clear view of her face. It was flushed, excited:

"Oh, good-ee! Malcolm!"

She clasped her hands together and jumped for joy like a child. And then she looked up at him with an expression of wonder. It was as if she had seen a god. It was the way I had felt when I first saw her. Something inside me felt dead and cold and leaden, and then began the surge and surge of pain. I looked past her to Tom, to see if he felt it too, but there was nothing except pleasure and welcome in his most readable and unsubtle face. He came forward:

"Hullo, Malcolm. What's your poison?"

It was a little too casual, perhaps, but it hid no raging jealousy; rather, I thought, it was an expression of pride—pride that he was on such intimate terms with this godlike being that he could receive him in so informal a way. Malcolm advanced into the room. As if we were indeed the chorus on the stage, we all made way for him. With a dramatic sweep his arms came forward. He held them stretched out and slightly bent at the elbows. Lying across them was the most magnificent bouquet of roses that I have ever seen in my life—bloom upon bloom, some in bud, some in full glory. Crimson velvety petals, silky yellow, delicate pink, matchless white. It was an outsize bouquet—overwhelming, an excess of ostentation. It would not have disgraced an offering to the most spoilt of prima donnas. And it must have cost the earth.

He held them for a moment outstretched for all the room to see, and then with a ballet dancer's poise and grace, sank on to bended knee and offered them to Judy.

"Beauty for beauty," he said, smiling up at her.

It should have been theatrical and absurd. But it wasn't. To my mind it was terrifying.

Judy took the flowers and buried her face in them, exclaimed "Ouch!" as a thorn brushed her cheek, and then she blushed as crimson as the roses. Malcolm got effortlessly to his feet and flicked an imaginary speck of dust from his knee.

"Glad you like them," he said in an offhand manner. "The usual please, Tom. Plenty of soda."

I looked at Malcolm, and the pain surged and surged, and my heart began to race, and I felt murder. You're mad, man, mad, I thought as my glance rested on Tom happily pouring out Scotch. And then I looked round at Dennis and Harry who were standing near to me, and at Liz beside them, and at Tom's friend and Judy's friend who were near the door, and they all seemed to be shrunk and shabby and withered and smaller than life, and it seemed to me that something of my own feelings was reflected in the eyes of each. And then my eyes lighted on the table full of little gifts, on the modest vases of tulips and irises and rather faded freesias, and I thought of the shillings that had been spent, by people who hadn't many shillings to spare, in kindness and goodwill to bring their homage to Judy's beauty. For a second my rage was such that I could have seized the roses and thrown them to the floor and trampled them underfoot. And then my eyes smarted and I could have wept—wept at the insult to all these harmless people, wept at the look Judy had given him, wept with self-pity because she would never look thus at me. I bent for a moment over the cookbook, which I was still holding, in order to hide my face, and when I looked up again I saw that Malcolm had taken a glass from Tom and was looking around the room. The cold blue eyes rested fleetingly on me and then moved on.

"Tom—introduce me please. Who do I know? Who *don't* I know?"

I could detect no hint of his origin or background from the light, supercilious tones.

Tom began to bustle about—a faithful lackey. "You know Liz, and you've met Susan, haven't you?—and our neighbours . . ."

Malcolm was not listening to him. He was staring at Judy in exaggerated horror. "*Dar*-ling! That frock!" He put a hand across his eyes and then removed it. "*When* will you learn? *Not* on you!—and *not* with diamanté. Please. It's too much. Another whisky please, Tom."

I held my breath and I thought I heard a slight horrified gasp from Liz beside me. My eyes went to Tom. His back was turned to me as he poured out from the bottle. There was nothing to be judged from it. It was Liz who exploded:

"Well, *I* think Judy's dress is super, and as a matter of fact that brooch is Tom's birthday present to her and I think it's super too, and who the bloody hell d'you think *you* are, bursting in like this like the bloody great queen you are except that you'll never make it, and with your *bloody* great roses . . ."

"Liz, *please!*" It was Judy who spoke. She had laid the bouquet on the table and was standing beside Liz, touching her arm and looking down at her with a face now pale and with eyes that looked near tears. "Please, Liz. It's my birthday."

"No, don't stop her," said Malcolm. "I'm enjoying this. Her range of adjectives is somewhat limited, but no doubt we shall learn some new language in a moment."

"You swine! You filthy sod! You . . ."

Liz was screaming and her hands were upraised and bent into claws. Hysterical, unbalanced; they so often are, I thought sadly. I didn't like her, but at the moment my sympathies were entirely on her side. Of course she was playing straight into Malcolm's hands, but she was also, paradoxically enough, easing the tension by acting out what the rest of us were feeling but dared not express.

Malcolm looked at her unmoved and then shook his head. "You really must learn to control yourself, Elizabeth. Your genius is not so great that it entitles you to ignore all the social niceties."

Liz swung on her heel and slammed out of the room.

Imperceptibly, sympathy had swung round towards Malcolm. After all, whatever the provocation, one does not make scenes at people's birthday parties. We were relieved at Liz's departure. We came out of our frozen attitudes and began to move about the room.

"Oh Malcolm!" Judy looked her most melting. "They're so absolutely gorgeous! I've never seen anything like it in my life—and I haven't a vase to put them in."

"They won't *last*, darling. They're only hothouse."

"But I must put them in water," wailed Judy. "Tom—can't you think of anything?"

Tom still had his back to the rest of us. He seemed to be having great difficulty in opening one of the bottles. He tugged clumsily at the corkscrew and it came away with only half the cork attached to it.

"Damn."

"Let's have a go, old chap."

Malcolm was at his side, polite, helpful, man-to-man. Tom looked up and I thought I saw a disappointed, reproachful look on his face. Malcolm said something in a low voice that I did not catch, and then Tom spoke again. I watched them closely from my vantage point by the window. Malcolm had his back to me, but as they talked I saw Tom's sulky expression fade away. Silly young fool, I thought angrily; he's got you where he wants you. A handsome apology, no doubt, and a couple of press tickets for a show he doesn't want to see, or whatever other crumbs of bribery he throws out for the young moron. He was so obviously trying to placate Tom that it occurred to me that the dramatic entry was not a normal function, but was put on specially for the benefit of the guests—perhaps even specially for my benefit. And the goading of the wretched Liz—was this to show me what might happen to me? And the insolent behaviour to Judy and Tom—to show how strong was his hold on them, how easily they could be brought round?

I found myself moving towards the door, so full of fury that I forgot to think myself into my role. Judy caught me by the arm:

"Oh, Miss Wentworth, aren't they gorgeous? Did you ever see such roses! But I must put them in water. You haven't a big vase, have you?"

"I know, I'll fetch a bucket," said Dennis, and disappeared. Judy continued to cling to me. She was still very agitated, and I found it some compensation that she came to me for moral support. But there was no chance of escape. Dennis was back in a minute or two and the roses were arranged to show their gleaming heads above the smudgy blue plastic. Judy apologised for the makeshift vase, but Malcolm laughed:

"Positively original, my dear."

"Really?" I said. "A common enough sight, surely, on the floor of any florist's shop."

Even as I spoke I could have kicked myself. Of all the crazy, crazy things to do—to step forward into Malcolm's attention with a stupid little remark like that. To stay in the background—that had been my resolve, my only hope. And yet here was I, rising like a fish, differing only from Liz in my greater maturity and self-restraint. With all my heart and mind I wished the silly words unsaid. In every respect but one, Malcolm was different from what I had expected. But that one was the most important of all: he was dangerous.

"How right you are," he said, and smiled at me charmingly. "How foolish can one get in striving after the incongruous—the unexpected. You must be—no, Judy, let me guess—you are Miss—Wentworth?"

The hesitation in speaking the name held for me an

alarming significance. Involuntarily my eyes dropped to my left hand which held a wineglass, seeking the reassurance that the third finger was indeed ringless. I felt rather than saw that his eyes followed mine, and fear seized me, and every face in the room seemed cold and hostile and heavy with accusation. It was incredible that I could respond in a natural manner.

"That's right. I live next door. I'm afraid I've only heard you spoken of by your Christian name, Mr. . . ."

"Oh, call me Malcolm. Everyone does."

I was as stumped by this remark as one usually is. Was I supposed to respond with "Call me Mary"?

"You're working at the B.M., aren't you?" he continued in a friendly manner.

"That's right," I said again, amazed at my outward calm while my heart was racing and my will seemed paralysed.

"May one ask? Or is it very hush?"

"Not particularly. Only copying some documents for a study of the relations between Parliament and the press."

"Oh really? That's rather up my street. Any particular period? And any particular emphasis that you intend to give?"

We were standing in the centre of the room; the party was once more conversing in small groups and Tom was dispensing drinks. Only Judy stood near us, looking happily from my face to Malcolm's and back again.

"I'm not writing it myself," I said. "I'm devilling for someone else."

The words came out unbidden. Too late I realised that I should have prepared a convincing lie, headed him off, refused to be forced into a corner. It was too late now; I was mesmerised, I had no power to dissemble.

"What a bore for you," he said sympathetically. "You do all the work and someone else has all the fun and gets all the kudos. No—don't tell me, let me guess who is likely to be interested in the press and Parliament at the moment." He stared frowningly at his glass.

Judy looked at him in childish admiration of his knowledge and his cleverness.

I looked at him with the hopeless certainty of a trapped animal about to be mauled to death.

"Of course," he said at last, "it must be old Parry Barlow—he's about due for another of his magnum opus— opi—opuses?—what on earth *is* the plural?—my Latin was never very efficient."

Very considerate, I thought bitterly; a little bit of chitchat to allow me time to recover from the one shock in order that he may enjoy all the more administering the next. Let the terrified creature go for a moment and then pounce again. Oh, had I only had the sense to invent a plausible tale! How hatred and fear had shattered my judgement! To link me with Parry Barlow—this was a first sure step to detection. Denial would be hopeless, for he was obviously well informed. To pass it off lightly was my only course.

"Yes, it is Professor Barlow," I said as brightly as I could. "That's very clever of you to guess. Do you know him?"

"Only on paper. I suppose he must be the most inaccessible recluse that British scholarship has produced for many a year. It's always been a mystery to me how he manages to overcome his phobia of human contact sufficiently to obtain the essential material for his books. Are you ever permitted to approach him? Or is it all done by post?"

"Oh—it's all done by post," I said casually, and then I could stand no more, and I swallowed the rest of my drink, and with a pretence of wanting to put down my glass I was able to create a general movement of people in the room and to escape from Malcolm and stand with Dennis and Harry near the door.

"I've got an awful head," I murmured to them after a minute of seeming to listen, but not knowing in the least what they said. "Would you make my excuses if I disappear?"

A moment later I was outside on the landing, ashamed of an exit that was as clumsy as, if less violent than, that of Liz, who was no doubt skulking upstairs in her room. I would have liked to do the same, but did not dare. A thin wall and a feeble Yale lock was no defence against Malcolm. I could sense him standing there, in temporary frustration because he had allowed his victim too great a rein; but already joyfully anticipating the next little cat and mouse act.

I found myself trembling uncontrollably, and my whole body felt suffused with a mixture of horror and rage that nauseated and almost choked me. For a short while I stood there, my mind refusing to direct my limbs into any action that would bring me ease and turn my way into a safer refuge, and then I walked slowly downstairs to the front door and out on to the pavement, and the cool evening air, so far from calming and restoring me, only added the shiverings of chill to those of fear.

In such a condition I moved along, habit directing my footsteps, until I was in the corner of Russell Square nearest to the British Museum. There I found a bench and sat down, staring unseeing at the concrete bowls of tulips and the low shrubs and the occasional solitary student walking by. And gradually the arrangements of colours—pink tulips, green leaves, dirty grey—began to impress themselves upon my mind and take on a meaning and I became once more an individual human consciousness, aware of the names and the nature of the objects around. Like the view from my window. If all life could be shrunk and canalised into the immediately perceptible; if only consciousness could be that of an animal or a young child, with no awareness of past or future, no regrets and memories, no fears and hopes—I imagined it to be thus, and found a momentary peace. And then the thought came: but that would be to live in a prison cell. And then instantly, blinding and overwhelming, came the further thought: it could have been my fate, it very nearly was my fate.

But would it have been so much worse than my present life? I should have been safe from such as Malcolm. I should have received food and drink; I should have been constantly among women—and that ought to have suited me, I thought bitterly. Perhaps I should have had a cell-mate—a hideous, gin-soaked old hag, toothless, foul-tongued, misshapen with child-bearing. I began to laugh at myself, a little madly. One would hardly expect to find something like Judy Prescott in Holloway jail.

But I don't want to harm her, I begged, and it was the judge at the Assizes to whom I was pleading; I would not wish her any harm, I only want to see her now and then, to warm myself in the glow of her beauty and dream of youth and of being her lover. She knows nothing of it; she never will know; neither she nor her marriage shall suffer anything through me.

I found myself crying. I believe I had cried in the courtroom. Not at that moment, oddly enough, when the summing-up of the prosecuting counsel reached its climax, but earlier on, when old Professor Barlow had stood there in the witness box giving evidence of my good character. It was the sight of him, so frail, so nervous, so desperately shy, standing up there before all those people and speaking the words which, I later learnt, had done as much as anything to acquit me, it was this sight that had moved me beyond endurance. Poor old chap; how he had hated it. I really believe that he had suffered more than I had.

The faces of the judge, and the old professor, and the court officials and the anonymous listeners, receded; the black and brown of the courtroom dissolved and re-formed into pink and green and grey. The moisture on my face seemed more than could be accounted for by tears, and I became aware that it was raining. It was also growing dark.

I was sitting on a bench in a public garden in my thin cocktail frock on a cool and damp evening in late spring and I didn't know where to go because I had no home.

I cried a little more, from self-pity, and had the fantasy that I was indeed down-and-out, a social outcast. Perhaps the Salvation Army would give me shelter; perhaps the police would come and take me in. That's likely, I sneered at myself, with your model dress and your crocodile handbag with a nice wad of five-pound notes in the wallet. Take yourself off to a comfortable hotel—leave the over-strained charities to those who really need them. But to be alone in a hotel bedroom, unknown, uncared for, a number in the register, the characterless, featureless raw material of the hotel industry, the impersonal means whereby others earned their daily bread—this was to step right over the edge. A short paragraph in the evening paper the following day would be my epitaph: "Body of unidentified woman found in hotel bedroom; bottle of sleeping tablets removed by the police."

It might come to that some day. But not yet. Please God, not yet. I *did* have a home. Home was a shabby Georgian house in a Bloomsbury square, with a poor old crippled caretaker in the basement, an ever-changing assortment of Indian students in the attics, and a few ordinary people in between—people who had good points and bad points; of whose loves and hates and private fears and hopes I knew nothing, but whose faces I knew, whose step on the stairs and whose taste in radio and television programmes I knew—the Prescotts with their thrillers, Dennis and Harry with their Third Programme concerts, Dr. Strangeways with the steady relentless drone of the current affairs commentaries. It made me nostalgic to think of them. And they knew as little and as much of me, and accepted me on those terms. For one coming slowly back to the world of human relationships, convalescing from the illness of total isolation, it was enough to say "Good morning," and "Yes,

aren't the petunias coming on well?" and "Could you give
me some change for the laundrette?" And, of course, to
look at Judy and dream.

For two whole weeks I had known something like peace.
I liked my shabby room. I was not going to be driven away.
Could I have been mistaken? Could my own consciousness
and fears alone have been to blame? That Malcolm was an
evil character I felt sure; but he might not be specifically
aiming at me—his behaviour towards me might simply be
an instance of his general liking to probe for people's
weaknesses. Or perhaps the Prescotts had been irritating
him by their praise of me and he wanted to score over me.
For a moment this seemed possible, and then I remembered
the look he had given me when he asked if I knew Professor
Barlow. Of course he had guessed; he must have guessed.

I tried to force my thoughts into a logical chain, to weigh the
possibilities of discovery. But my mind was exhausted; it
could not deal with it. I wanted to be home. I got up from the
bench and walked slowly back through the gardens, hugging
the short jacket of my frock around me in a pretence of
protection against the rain. When I came out into Southampton
Row I turned into a little Italian café that stayed open very late
and ordered a meal that I did not want at all. But the coffee was
good and I sipped it gratefully, under the incurious eyes of the
little brown man behind the counter. He was used to far odder
sights than a short, dark, middle-aged woman in a wet party
frock and with a distraught manner. There are many lost souls
in Bloomsbury, many strangers alone and fearful and far from
home. I felt, as I sat there, the burden of them all, of all
outcasts condemned to stand outside in the darkness and see in
the lighted windows the life and gaiety and happiness within.
And gradually there came to me the calmness of despair, and
I walked around the streets until I could go no further, and then
I crept back to the house as if in a dream, and all the windows
were in darkness and my room was empty and dark and quiet
and cold and it welcomed me like the grave.

4

The heavily drugged sleep held me prisoner, even though my eyes had once opened and found the familiar view. It was lost again and I was in limbo. There was a faint tap on the door and a gentle plop and a rustle as my *Sunday Times* slid from Tom's hand to await my arising. I tried to move my limbs but they were leaden. How many pills had I taken? I could not remember. But certainly more than I should have, and on top of alcohol too. I pushed the bedclothes aside a little way and then once more succumbed.

Eons later there was a sharper knock. I was fully awake, able to move, but disorientated. My eyes sought the low casements of my Cornish home; my legs wanted the bedroom door to be on the right of the bed and not the left; my mind knew it was Sunday morning and was puzzled at the knock, because our daily help did not come on a Sunday, Robert could not get up without my help, and Estelle would never come to my room. And yet it must be Estelle. There was a rising excitement in me as I slipped on my light dressing-gown. But in the very movement time and place returned, and I stood groping and struggling while a second knock came, even louder, peremptory.

Judy was dressed in her oldest clothes and had not yet

43

pinned up her hair. She had my newspaper and my carton of milk in her hand.

"Oh—Miss Wentworth, I'm terribly sorry—did I wake you?"

I was rubbing my eyes to hide a sudden uncontrollable twitching of my face.

"I'm awfully sorry," she went on, "but it's nearly one o'clock and we hadn't heard you move and I was so worried because you weren't well last night. . . ."

She did indeed look very worried. Were it possible to imagine her other than perfect, I should say that tension and pallor were marring her beauty. I blinked at her—I was indeed very dazed—and her eyes opened further to dissolve in that infinite softness which only she could command as she put a hand on my arm and directed me back to bed.

"Oh you poor thing! You *are* ill! I was sure you were—you'd never have left so suddenly if you hadn't been really ill—although I was so afraid that you were disgusted by Liz, but she can't help it, you know, and doesn't really mean it—look, you get back into bed and I'll bring you anything you like. Or do you think you ought to have the doctor?"

I allowed myself to be guided back between the sheets. Half my consciousness was still in the past, dreaming that it was Estelle who was bending over me but resentfully knowing that she never would have done so, and the other half of my mind was very much alive and critically in the present, thinking that the angelic Judy would be a tactless and irritating companion to one suffering from sickness or distress.

"It's this wretched migraine," I lied, though my appearance was no doubt giving my words the truth, "it hits me quite out of the blue and there's no cure but to sleep it off. I've taken some stuff for it."

"Are you sure there's nothing I can do?" She looked disappointed. Evidently she had been fancying herself in the nursing role, because she looked around the room and I had an unpleasant suspicion that she was going to insist upon dusting and hoovering and spraying with disinfectant in order to make it suitable for an invalid to lie in. I got rid of her at last by saying that I should simply love some tea and toast in about an hour's time. How this girl does corrupt my speech, I thought as she left the room; having started off with a subtly mocking imitation of her manner of talking, I now found myself falling into it automatically. What a commonplace, stupid little creature it was! Estelle, at least, had had brains, had been a worthy opponent. Opponent? Was love, then, of necessity a battle? All's fair in love and war, I murmured as I dozed off.

I awoke feeling weak but rested. My reason was functioning perfectly and so was my memory. I had a clear picture of my panic rush from Judy's party and of what had gone before. So he can't have said anything yet, I thought, or she would not behave to me like this. I considered the matter quite dispassionately; the emotion normally attendant upon thought had been temporarily deadened by the drug. Enzyme inhibitors? What was it they called those modern chemicals which can relieve depression and mania by blocking the flow of excessive feeling and allowing the detached intellect to take control? I could not remember for certain, but that was just how I felt, although in fact what I had swallowed was nothing other than old-fashioned barbiturate.

When Judy came I was surprised to find that I really wanted the tea. She drew a chair up to my bedside and poured it out. It slopped into the saucer, of course, and there were more floating tea-leaves in the cup than anyone else ever succeeded in producing, but it tasted good, all the same. I smiled at her gratefully.

"You must have thought me rude last night," I said, "but these things come on suddenly and affect the eyesight, you know. I honestly don't think I could have found my way out if I'd waited another moment. I do hope Harry explained."

"Oh yes—or rather he just said he thought you were feeling ill. I came and knocked later on, but I don't think you can have heard, or maybe you felt too bad or just couldn't be bothered to answer the door."

It was quite genuine, I felt sure. They did not know I had left the house. They believed that I had lain there ill in my room while the party drew to a close.

"It was a lovely party," I went on, "and what an interesting person your friend Malcolm is." Take care, I said to myself; don't overdo the enthusiasm.

Her face lighted up for a moment. "Yes, isn't he? I knew you would get on—he's awfully clever—I don't know why he bothers with me and Tom—we're terribly ignorant, and he knows absolutely loads of people."

I thought it wisest to nod and say nothing.

"You know, Miss Wentworth," she went on, "I've never been able to talk to my mother—she's a bit jealous of me, I think." This was said with a measure of pride in her own psychological insight. "I hope you don't mind—I know I haven't known you long, but I do think you are so *sensible*, and I feel I can trust you and I'd much rather talk to you than to anyone my own age, and although you're not married you're so well balanced that you quite easily might have been—and I feel that if you'd ever had a daughter . . ."

She paused a moment, and my hand holding the teacup jerked. I had been within a hair's breadth of saying it aloud—"But I did have a step-daughter." These emotion-inhibitors were doing their work only too well. Think, woman, think. A gentle snub, and a hint of returning migraine? Would that shut her up? No, not our Judy. Besides, I had an uncontrollable curiosity to know what she was going to say.

"Of course there's absolutely nothing in it—I mean he was Tom's friend before mine, and we've often thought he was a queer—not that there's ever been any sign of it but he doesn't seem to have any girl friends—not in the normal way, that is, although he knows heaps of women and they're always chasing him—fashion writers and interior decorators and journalists—*you* know—all that lot that write frightfully clever articles in the colour supplements—but it doesn't mean anything because Liz says lots of them are Lesbians themselves—where was I?—oh yes, Malcolm giving me presents. He's just *like* that, you know. He's always giving Tom things too—a perfectly super tie—did you see it? Likes to show off a bit. Well, don't we all? And he was an actor at one time. I should think he'd be awfully good, wouldn't you? He can't help it and it doesn't mean a thing and Tom knows that and he's never minded before—not in the least—so I don't know what's come over him now."

Her mouth drooped in injured innocence. I had no doubt that, for all its embarrassing ramifications, Judy's conventional little soul secretly loved to receive out-size bouquets of roses in a dramatic manner at the hands of a gorgeous-looking man, and the suspicion that he had no sexual interest in women cast a glow of purity over the act and added to the pleasure. And she liked, too, to spin a little web of intrigue around herself. There lay her vanity—not to be openly admired, adored and worshipped, but to feel that her beauty had created a complicated situation. A harmless piece of self-dramatisation perhaps, but for me, desperately vulnerable as I was, her little games were full of dangers.

"I thought you were all on such good terms that this sort of thing could not arise," I said mildly, knowing full well that every word I uttered would be carried straight back to Malcolm, and feeling quite sure that, for all her seeming concern, she was not seriously worried about Tom.

That stumped her and she tried another tack: "Did *you* like my brooch, Miss Wentworth?"

I thought rapidly. "Yes, I did. It's very pretty in itself but I do agree that it would look better on another dress."

"Well, if *you* liked it—and you've got super taste—even Malcolm thought so." This was evidently intended to be the height of compliment. I could find nothing to say. "He liked you awfully," she went on with a rush, "he thought you were very elegant and a bit aloof and mysterious—like a celebrity in disguise—and he couldn't think what you were doing in a mucky hole like this except that if you'd taken the room by letter from a distance of course you wouldn't know what it was like."

I was glad I was lying propped up in bed, for once again I felt weak with apprehension. "But I like it here," I said. "It's got character. You know, Judy, I've had rather a dull life, always among elderly people, and this is the first time I've been free, and it's rather fun to be a bit Bohemian for a change."

"Oh yes, I can understand *that*. My mother and father— you should just see them. It's always what will the neighbours think and who's bought what kind of new car—you get sick of it. But it's not *you* really. I mean you're so different. Look what you've done to your room. It's just the same as ours and yet it looks—it looks . . ." She searched for a word, gazing wistfully around her, the rosy lips slightly parted in the most tantalising manner. I shut my eyes for a moment and gripped my hands together under the sheets. "What can I do with ours?" she went on. "Do you think one of those Heal's lampshades would help?"

"I'll think about it, Judy," I said, "but please not now. I'm still very tired."

When she had gone I slumped back against the pillows and closed my eyes. I should have to go. There was no hope of hiding now. To become friendly with the Prescotts had been risky enough, with the way that I felt about Judy, and with her inquisitiveness, and with the threatening shadow of Malcolm ever present. But to be drawn into rivalry with him, to be quoted at him as he was quoted at me, played off one against the other—this was madness. For all her adoration, Judy would be less than human if she were not a little hurt by his scorn of her taste. She could not fight back herself; I was to do it for her.

Oh Judy, if you only knew what you were doing to me! You hold my life in your smile, my fate is in your hands. I am doubly ensnared—held fast by your beauty, caught by the trap you have dragged me into. If only I could tell you! If I could tell you, you would surely pity me.

5

All evening I lay thus, barely conscious of the colours in the window frame and the rattling of crockery and the rise and fall of the television sound from next door. Sometimes I was hopeless, sometimes it seemed to me that I might yet be safe.

Malcolm had recognised me. I had no doubt of that. I looked different now—I was much thinner, my hair was short and openly greying and I made up my eyes to look dark and my mouth to look small. The newspaper photographs at the time had been far from perfect, and for the average casual reader I was a seven-day wonder, long since forgotten. But for a journalist—and with all his artistic pretensions that was what Malcolm seemed basically to be—it was a different matter. He knew me. What was he going to do? Would he keep quiet? Had he a heart? No. Again and again no. What creature with any feeling could have burst in on a party like that, deliberately, offensively overshadowing all the harmless little people already gathered there. They had resented and disliked him. They were unbiased judges; they knew.

I could expect no mercy. And I had, all unwittingly, hit at his weakness, his vanity. For that was all the Prescotts meant to him—an endless supply belt to his insatiable,

all-consuming vanity. But where there is vanity there is
weakness too. Could I but find the weakness, take the
offensive and attack quickly while I had courage left, before
my unreasoning terror of him had paralysed my own will.
Or should I try to bribe him? I had money enough—far, far
more than I would ever know how to use. And he liked the
things that money could buy. I rose next morning with no
solution in my mind. I could make no decision; I was borne
by the tide.

For a week I remained thus. I did my work and slept and
ate, and avoided my neighbours as much as I could. Every
evening I walked the streets aimlessly, thoughtlessly, killing
the time until the moment arrived when two small pink
capsules brought temporary relief. If Malcolm would only
go away. If he would only quarrel with the Prescotts and
visit them no more. Could I perhaps fan Tom's jealousy—if
indeed he were jealous? Could I arouse that smouldering
passion of possession in him of which I had once caught so
fleeting a glimpse?

It was the only hope, a feeble one, and full of risks. And
it did not comfort me for long.

On the Saturday morning I met Tom carrying two great
bags of shopping. "Judy's a lucky girl," I said. "Do you
always do this chore?"

"Oh, I don't mind," he replied. " 'Smatter o' fact"—and
his pudgy face went pinker than ever under the sandy hair—
" 'smatter o' fact I like it because Judy's inclined to forget
things and it means I can choose my own supper."

I laughed. "That's an advantage, certainly."

"Not that she doesn't do her best," he said hastily, "and
she works jolly hard at her job and hasn't much time."

"You both work very hard," I said, playing for time and
wondering how on earth I was going to carry out my
purpose. "And after all, one can't expect the best cook in
the world and the prettiest girl to be combined in one
person, can one?"

"Good Lord, no. And I'm so lucky—I can't think why she ever looked at me."

Neither can I, I echoed mentally, but aloud I said jokingly: "You'll have to keep an eye on her, Tom. You don't want some predatory chap trying to whisk her away."

He frowned a little and then said: "Judy's not like that at all. She's never been interested in other men. She didn't have all that many boy friends even before we were married."

Didn't she indeed, I said to myself, and my thoughts began to race beyond my control.

"I'm glad for both your sakes," I said aloud, "and I hope you'll always be very happy, and I hope your supper will be a success."

"Oh, this is for tomorrow," he replied. "We're going out tonight—Malcolm's taking us to that new Spanish restaurant in Charlotte Street. And then we're going to the Arts Theatre."

It was hopeless. It always would be. I could picture the three of them in cramped and cosy intimacy, Tom and Judy puzzling over the menu, Malcolm directing the waiters with a lordly air. It was intolerable; it was beyond endurance. And this creature knew my secret.

"Well, have a nice time," I said, and felt as if the words were choking me, and then some force outside myself took over and led me on: "You must join me one evening if you like Continental cookery—I found quite a nice little place in Chelsea the other day."

Horrified at myself, I awaited his beaming acceptance. I was even deeper, far deeper in it than I had been before. I spent the rest of the weekend sitting in news cinemas, or walking, walking. I dared not sit in my room for fear the knock at the door might come; I dreaded to go home. When I had to leave my room, I first listened carefully from just inside the door to make sure that there was nobody on the stairs. I thought I was safe on the Monday morning, since most of the tenants left early for work, but as I stepped on to the landing there was a rapid flurry of footsteps and Liz appeared suddenly beside me, all thin black-clad arms and legs, like some great whirling insect. She had been lying in wait; our ways to work lay together and I could not escape her. We descended the stairs.

"What a lovely morning," I said.

She gave me a disdainful look and did not trouble to reply. We walked in silence.

"What d'you think of Malcolm?" she asked a few minutes later.

My heart jumped. "The Prescotts' friend?" I said carefully. "I've barely met him. I left their party soon after you did. I had a blinding migraine and could barely stand up."

"Don't blame you," she said abruptly and swung her battered portfolio round so that it banged against the railings. "Filthy swine," she muttered under her breath.

"Why do you dislike him so much? He seemed a bit theatrical, but basically harmless, surely."

"Oh, I dunno. He's—he's mucky. He isn't a straight queer like the others. He has to muck around with women— though I'll swear he never made one in his life. I'll tell you what"—and as the thought struck her she swung her portfolio again and gave a little jump so that with all her paint-stained trews and her lanky hair she suddenly looked very young and innocent—"I know what he's like. Did you ever see Nigel Reeves?" She named a famous matinée idol of my own youth. "I saw him once when I was a kid—he was past it really but still a box office draw. My parents loved it. One of those treacly sagas—he's so handsome and modest and she's so sweet and inaccessible. He could sing all right—I'll hand him that one. There he was belting out I'll worship you from afar with his buttery wig and his toothpaste grin—the bloody old queen! Ugh! Made you sick. But that's Malcolm."

For a fleeting moment I saw Malcolm not as the dangerous antagonist who had guessed my secret and held my fate in his hands, but as the ageing singer, clinging with weakening grasp to the slippery heights of fame. "That's rather pathetic," I said, and for a minute or two we walked along without speaking. Then she looked at me with a sly sideways glance under her hanging hair:

"If you're worrying that he's got designs on Judy," she said, "you can forget it. It's all perfectly pure—pure as snow—pure as hell." She looked away, and then back at me again.

"It did strike me as a bit embarrassing for Tom," I said mildly.

She looked at me again, full in the face this time, with a contemptuous stare. I met it unmoved. We were much of a height. Then she coloured a little, bit her lip and looked away. I was pleased, triumphant with the heady knowledge that I still had the power to snub and reprove with a look alone, but I was more terrified than ever because I knew I had made an enemy. Lovers or adversaries—for we who are born as we are there is no middle way. She could do me harm; she would talk to Judy.

"I've seen Nigel Reeves on the stage once or twice," I said casually, "and I think there is a certain likeness. But I wouldn't call him a great brain, whereas the Prescotts' friend seemed to me to be highly intelligent."

"Oh Lord, yes. He knows his stuff—and where to get it too."

"Where to get it? Do you mean he is a drug pedlar?" I was very much the shocked and ignorant middle-aged woman.

She laughed harshly—it was not unlike Judy's laugh. "Nothing so obvious. I only meant he knows where the money is. Look at those damned roses. Five quid, wouldn't you say? And his clothes. He doesn't pay for *those* out of half a column in the weeklies once in a while and a bit of crime reporting on the side!"

She was contemptuous again, and this time I did not try to stare her down. She could think me a square and a prig and a hypocrite whom it was her pleasure to shock and despise; but my own thoughts had formed the word "blackmail" and I could not keep it to myself.

I tried to speak in character, with an air of distaste: "Are you trying to suggest that he may be a—blackmailer?"

"I dunno." She was childish again. "I wouldn't put it past him."

"Well, he certainly won't get much change out of the Prescotts." I was very brisk.

"Oh Lord no. Not *them*." She spat out the last word.

We were nearing the end of our ways together, and I was glad of this, for there was arising once again within me the sickening swell of fear; I was longing and yet dreading to know more, but I knew that I could no longer keep up the impersonal note, and were I to ask any more questions I should surely give myself away.

"Well, I'll be leaving you here," I said feebly as we reached Russell Square. She gave me another of the sideways glances, said: "If you really want to find out about Malcolm, you'd better ask Dr. Strangeways—they've been getting pally lately," and hitching up her portfolio under her arm, she ran off in the direction of the Senate House.

I walked on a few yards and then sat down on a bench. The arrangement of forms and colours in front of my eyes told me that this was the very spot where I had sat after the party. I was not in the mindless panic that I had been in then, but I was quite frightened enough. Crime reporter and possible blackmailer. It could not be much worse. I held in my lap the little briefcase that contained my working notes, and the firm and soft feel of the leather reminded me that I had some claim to academic ability and must use my powers of orderly reasoning to help myself now.

I'll start with the very worst, I thought, as if laying out the plan for an essay. Suppose Malcolm was at my trial and has recognised me. Then, assuming that he is *not* a kind-hearted person who will quietly keep his knowledge to himself, there are three possibilities. One, he will demand money in return for silence. Two, he will expose me. Three, he will continue to play cat and mouse with me indefinitely. Alternative one was the least alarming; alternative three the most. It might, in fact, be almost a relief if he were to come to me and say straight out that he knew it all and to state his price. I had the money—Robert's money. There was no one left to inherit. I had no need of it myself.

I began to visualise the scene, myself contemptuous, cynical, unmoved, more like the blackmailer in behaviour than like the victim.

"Are you sure five hundred is enough?" I would say. "I can easily up it ten per cent if you're short."

He could not possibly know how much I had; details of that, at least, had not been given at my trial. For all I cared he could have a thousand a year for life if it would give me security and . . .

And what? Why, apart from the fact that I was trying to forget the past and start life again, was I so horrified at the idea of the second alternative—of exposure? I had been acquitted; there was no question of re-trial; it would be unpleasant were people to know, but it would not be the end of everything. Why, then, this overwhelming horror at the thought?

The answer came pat: because you have fallen in love with Judy. Because to see her glorious beauty every day and have her respect and admire you—to have her, with all her clumsiness, wish tenderly to care for you—this has become the very reason for your existence, the focus of all your dreams, that little core of hope—or rather of feeling—that every human being needs for survival. For we can live without love and we can live without hope, but some sort of feeling we must have; and if we are unlucky, we must make do with the feeling of hate—hatred alone can keep us going.

Indifference in others towards ourselves we can endure; indifference in ourselves towards others is the killer.

I cannot leave Judy. My hands stroked the soft, firm leather of my little briefcase. My lovely flower, my rising sun, my beauty. Just to look at you, to watch those lips droop, those liquid eyes dissolve. No, I would not touch you. Never. I have only in my thoughts touched another woman lovingly. I could not do it in fact. It's a thing of the mind alone. That's what you don't understand, you stupid little beatnik Liz and all the others like you. You don't know what it is to love in pure fantasy of stroking that silken hair, caressing that lovely body, drifting with lips like a butterfly's wing over cheek and neck and throat.

As if I would ever make a move! Why, have I not been a married woman, have I not been held by my own dear husband in the embrace of love, dreaming the while of a body such as yours, Judy, and gaining through those dreams my own ecstasy? For what are human identities when they meet and dissolve in love? What does it matter who sets off the spark so long as he who deserves it feels the gift? It is a chain reaction whereby all may benefit. Why else has pornography—for such is its lowest form—persisted over the centuries, and will do so until the end of time? I have loved Robert truly; I have given him, in those few years, comfort and companionship and steady happiness such as he never knew with his first wife. I have given him the utmost of physical joy. That my release of feeling came only through my dreams of a girl's beauty—that was not known to him.

There was no hurt to him in it. It was my terrible misfortune, mine alone, that the beauty was that of his own daughter.

Estelle—Judy—Estelle. My eyes were half-closed and my hands stroked the soft and firm but yielding leather.

And then every nerve in my body was taut and tingling. Someone among the few passers-by had not only glanced at

me, but had looked and really seen me. Had seen not only
me but all my visions too. I felt stripped and naked; in the
dock once more. I stared along the path, first one way, then
the other. Walking rapidly towards Great Russell Street,
nearly out of the gardens now, was a familiar figure,
middle-aged, middle height, undistinguished. Frequently,
as I stood at my window, I had seen it turn the corner of our
square.

Dr. Strangeways, taking the shortest route to the British
Museum, had happened to glance at the bench and notice
that a fellow lodger was sitting there. He had seen me
looking a little distrait, perhaps, and had consequently felt
grateful not to have to stop and pass the time of day. But
that was all. The rest was my consciousness—my conscience. All he knew of me was that I was working in the
Manuscript Room. An intellectual sort of female in cheap
digs in Bloomsbury.

And so I was. Had I not been pursuing, with calm logic,
a chain of thought that was to determine my future behaviour? Alternative three—and my mind slipped neatly back
as if its meanderings had never been—alternative three was
the worst. The slow torture of wondering every day, every
minute, whether he knew, what he was going to do. Does
he? Doesn't he? Will he? Won't he? The agony of suspicion,
of apprehension, of waiting. A hint dropped here and there.
To the edge of the precipice—all but a leg let go—and then
the pulling back, slowly, every second a threat that the final
drop might yet come after all; perhaps a slip, a pretended
clumsiness, a quick retrieval, and then safety.

Safety until the next time. The torture with variations.
And then again. And again.

And I knew it, absolutely, with perfect clarity, as if
Malcolm had been standing there in front of me saying so.
Of course there would be no blackmail; of course there
would be no exposure; of course there would be only the
ever-present threat, the Sword of Damocles.

Unless I went away and never saw Judy again, which I could not bring myself to do. Or unless I told Judy myself.

Tell her! Tell Judy, that stupid, conventional, prudish little provincial girl? You're crazy. Tell her that you were tried for the murder of your husband by drowning just over a year ago—that you did it because you hated men, wanted your husband's money, didn't want him to know you had been making indecent advances to his daughter; that when she tried to save him, you let her drown too; that, acquitted due to lack of evidence, you nevertheless came out of it branded as a dangerous, wicked, unbalanced woman, a female sex maniac, a menace to all young girls.

Tell *Judy* all this? She'll never speak to you again; she'll feel sick at the sight of you. She'll be disgusted and nauseated to the bottom of her stupid little soul, the little fool.

The little fool. It made me so angry that I was so enslaved to the little fool that I jumped up, gripped my briefcase, and hurried along the path that Dr. Strangeways had taken a short while before. There was yet another alternative. I could behave coldly to Judy, withdraw myself; go on living there, but make it very plain to Judy and Tom—and thus to Malcolm too—that I was interested in none of them; unhurtable. That would blunt his weapon. I could act the part; I had learned to act.

I stopped short at the zebra crossing. It was too late. I had already shown myself too plainly. There was no reverting to the condition of tense and trembling isolation in which I had first arrived at the house in the square. There was no going back, I thought hopelessly, and I stepped on to the zebra without looking about me.

I felt the sickening, unbelievable hardness of the unyielding metal against my thigh before I heard the driver's shout, and then, by some extraordinary quirk of the angle of impact, I found myself straddled across the bonnet of the car, impaled obscenely upon a headlamp, with no worse damage done than a torn stocking and a light leather briefcase collecting dirt in the gutter.

A shaking hand helped me and a furious and terrified voice spoke: "Are you *sure* you're all right? Are you *sure?*"

"Perfectly sure. I am not in the least bit hurt. I am most desperately sorry—it was entirely my fault. Entirely."

I was not even aware of shock; I was conscious only of luxuriating in guilt and apology.

"Are you quite sure you're all right? Are you *sure?* Are you *sure?*"

Sure, sure, sure—it sounded in my ears like a sort of obsessional intermittent hiss. "Yes, I'm *sure* I'm all right. I'm *sure.*" My own voice took it up, a fainter echo.

Sure, sure, sure—it continued to buzz in my ears after I had sent the shaking driver on his way, and after the two or three people who had stopped to stare at us with dull and silent curiosity had gone away too.

"And there I was, stuck up on the bonnet like the mascot on a Rolls—except that it was a pretty ancient Ford Consul. Of all the daft things to do! I *was* so sorry for the driver . . ."

Whom was I talking to? I was making a story of it, digesting the shock, preparing in my mind for the actual therapeutic telling; for the gay self-deprecation, for the simultaneous alarming and reassuring of the listener, the equal evoking of sympathy and of admiration for cheerful conquest of fear.

I was talking to myself, I supposed. Like many another lonely widow, I was talking to a dead husband who had been the ever willing hearer of the mock-heroic exaggerated story, the cocktail party story; who had realised to the full the calming effect on strained nerves that such a narration produced. How strange it was, that Robert should so live on in me! After all my care to dispose of all his personal possessions, to avoid his friends, to think of him never.

I walked slowly across the great courtyard of the Mu-

seum, conscious now of a stiffness and incipient ache in my
left leg, and I built up a little fantasy that when I had pushed
my way through the revolving doors—which I disliked and
which always brought a little flicker of some incomprehen-
sible anxiety—I would see Robert standing there, waiting to
meet me, waiting patiently in his sightless way for me to
touch his arm and bring freedom to his limbs, and we would
go together to the snack bar, and there I would relate my
story of the zebra crossing.

It was bursting within me. The need to tell someone was
overwhelming. I had the crazy notion that it was sprouting
out of my head, like the "thinks" balloons in the comic
strips. I came into the Manuscript Room and walked as
usual to the reception desk. The short redhead with glasses
and a bad complexion was there. She glanced up at me and
I saw her expression change as I gripped the side of the desk
to hold myself upright.

"Are you feeling all right? You do look ill."

Her spectacles began to shatter and re-form as in a
kaleidoscope.

"I was nearly run over just now." My voice was steady
but a long way off. "Not hurt—but the shock's just come
on—have you a glass of water?"

She let me sit behind the desk with her and brought the
water. She listened with the calm gravity of an experienced
nurse while I wept a little and explained in short and
awkward sentences what had happened.

"Didn't you take his name and address?"

I shook my head. "It was all my fault."

"Not if you were on the crossing. It was your right of
way. He ought to have stopped. It's a serious offence. We'll
never cut down the accident figures if people are allowed to
get away with it like this."

Quietly reproving me for falling below the ideal critical
consumer standard, I thought; for being the passive under-
dog. Lives with a widowed mother, probably; goes to

evening classes in psychology and to humanist meetings.
Fabian Society most likely. Complacent, prudish. The
reverse side of the coin from antisocial, irresponsible youth.
I didn't know which was more boring. Youth. How dull and
dreary it was in its excesses, its intolerance. A blank
page—black or white. No subtlety, no mystery.

"It was such a shock that I'm afraid I hardly knew what
I was doing," I said to the earnest girl, and allowed her to
treat me with reproachful and condescending sympathy.

But all the time, underneath, my mind was still making a
bright social story of it, and the girl was part of the story,
and I was saying to my imaginary listener who had become
more real than the external world, who, rather than that
world, was the counter-force, the source of my ego-
awareness, I was saying: "I was rather grateful, really,
because she was very kind, and I don't know what I should
have done otherwise, but of course it soon passed over, and
I got down to work again . . ."

Got down to work again! My story had slipped into the
future. That part of my mind had taken on an independent
life of its own, was racing away out of control, trying to
chart the future, to draw its sting. With a tremendous effort
I managed to pull together all my strands of consciousness,
achieve the unity of place and time and experience.

"I must get to work now," I said.

"You don't look very fit for work. Hadn't you better go
home? Shall I get you a taxi?"

The earnest girl hovered over me. Her voice jarred,
became intolerable. I wanted to be alone with my internal
ghost, restoring my ego by relating my story to it, in my
own way, with no other reactions than those created and
controlled by my own imagination. And yet I knew that if
I were to venture alone into the street in this condition I
would be a danger to myself and to others.

"I'll go along to the snack bar," I said. "I'll feel better
after I've had some tea."

I had hard work persuading the girl not to come with me.

But by the time I had found a vacant place and collected my cup, the urgent need for solitude had dispersed, and I felt myself exhausted, drained of all thoughts and shaking a little with shock, incapable of any kind of action or decision. Should I go home by taxi? Should I stay and try to do some work? The alternatives weighed on me with equal pressure and there was no power left in me to make the choice. I might have sat there all day had not a man, with a murmured apology, taken a seat at the same table. It was with vast relief and a sensation of coming round from an anaesthetic, that I recognised Dr. Strangeways. Here was someone who could give me an identity, an address and a name. That was enough. This unknown man with whom I was barely on nodding terms was as good as any lifelong friend. Better, in fact. Had it been anyone who knew me from former times who had appeared at that moment, I would have collapsed completely, sobbed it all out, what had really taken place, and that little flicker of life and hope that had been aroused by Judy's beauty would have been extinguished for ever.

"Oh, hullo." Dr. Strangeways took a second glance at me to make sure of recognition before speaking. "I had forgotten you were working here."

"In Manuscripts," I replied. "Where are you?"

"Reading Room. The usual endless wait while they tour the shelves for the books you asked for days ago. But I can't get my material anywhere else, so I have to put up with it."

"Yes, it is a bore, isn't it?" I said sympathetically, and then we had reached the end of our powers of communication, and sipped our coffee in silence. I was no longer disorientated, but I was awkward and ill-at-ease, like a very raw first-year student meeting a tutor outside the lecture room. I could not tell, through the thick lenses of his glasses, whether he was looking at me or not. The non-speaking became oppressive. This is the sort of moment, I thought, when one makes one's most unforgettable social gaffes, when, desperate for something to say, one produces horrors of imbecility or tactlessness that make one shudder in memory for many years to come. What sort of absurdity was I about to give tongue to now? Or would his come out first? I waited fatalistically for the words to come from my lips.

But when they came they surprised me. "The Prescotts' friend—Malcolm what's-his-name," I said as if suddenly struck with a thought, and as I spoke I knew that this was what I had intended all along to say, "do you know him by any chance?"

"Not very well," he replied cautiously. "I've run across him once or twice lately. Why?"

"Well—I thought of asking him—and actually I'd like to ask you too if you have a moment—my job won't be lasting very much longer and I'm looking for more work of this kind. I thought of the Prescotts' friend because he seems to be the sort of person who gets around and knows a lot of people. That's the only way one finds this kind of work— personal contact and hearsay. It's useless going to an agency or making formal applications."

"What are your qualifications?"

I told him briefly. He was bored, resignedly courteous, and unsuspecting.

"I'll let you know if I hear of anything. Actually Malcolm might not be a bad person to ask. He seems to get around quite a bit."

"Is he approachable, do you know?—I mean, some people loathe being asked this sort of thing."

"I shouldn't think he'd mind. He seems quite approachable and is pretty good at approaching too, from what I can gather. I suppose journalists have to be. He might even want a bit of help himself. I don't know what he's got on at the moment, but I think he does quite a lot of rehashing famous criminal stories—sobstuff, new light on a murderess, that sort of thing. I should think it takes quite a lot of digging through old newspaper files. Of course that's probably hardly your line, although it's likely to pay better than valid research—you have to go to the big Foundations for that, and you say you don't want to. Is there anything the matter, Miss Wentworth? You don't look at all well."

I had put down my cup and slopped the liquid into the saucer because my hand shook so badly.

"I'm awfully sorry." My voice was shaking too. "It's just come over me again. I was knocked down by a car just now, and I thought I'd got over it but it keeps starting up again."

He was obliged to assume concern. I told the story once more, bored with it. "I think I really had better go home. It seems hopeless to try and work today."

I believe he helped me out of the building and hailed a taxi for me, but my journey was a blur. I reached my room at last and lay on my bed. I could not believe that I would ever rise from it again. My feeble attempts to get rid of Malcolm, to find out more about him, had reduced me to a condition of panic scarcely less paralysing than the one I had experienced after my first meeting with him, and I could see no light anywhere.

6

I lay low the rest of the week, doing no work, not going out at all except to slip round to the nearby shops when I was sure there was no one in the house who might see me; persuading myself that I needed time to get over the shock of the accident. I answered no knocks, went without my bath, stood listening at my door to make sure I could get there without being seen when I had to visit the lavatory on the half-landing. I crept around the room soundlessly, turning on the taps at the sink only when I was sure the Prescotts were out and would not hear the water running. On the Tuesday morning, when I was certain there was no one else in the house, I went down to the basement to tell the old caretaker that I was going away for a few days and to hold any mail. She had just returned from her painful trip to the shops and was sitting gasping for breath in her airless sitting-room. She nodded without interest.

I lived on black coffee and apples and cigarettes and sleeping pills. I lay on my bed and looked out of the window and saw nothing there.

On the Thursday morning I began to fear seriously for my sanity.

I had, on coming to London, decided not to seek out any former friends or acquaintances; not even those few who

67

had written to me with sympathy at the time of my trial and who might be expected to be kindly disposed towards me. But one contact I had promised myself. A very old couple, friends of my parents, who lived in Hampstead Garden Suburb, looked after by a German-born housekeeper nearly as old as themselves. As a child I had paid many long and happy visits to them; they remembered my birthday year by year, but still seemed to find it difficult to comprehend that I should grow older. They were further removed from my recent life and experiences than if they had been the other side of the world or on the moon; but at least they would recognise me, give me my true identity.

I spent two hours wondering whether or not to pack a small suitcase to take with me. It's running away, said one voice. You must give yourself a break to recover, said the other. For a while the two courses of action presented themselves in slow alternation—ding dong—a leisurely tolling church bell with its two notes. And then the vacillation speeded up—tick-tock, tick-tock—pack, don't pack; pack, don't pack—until the alternatives came no longer one after the other, but seemed to merge, or rather crash together, and I had decided on both courses of action at once. For a while I sat numb and unthinking, my mind drained from the effort of decision, and when it slowly began to function again, it was only to revert to the same pattern, first slow, then speeding up, only this time it was not a matter of actually making the decision, but of recalling the decision that I believed myself to have made before the interval.

I was dressed to go out and had money in my bag. I grabbed it up and left the room, slamming the door behind me, careless of whether I was seen or not, ran down the stairs and hailed a taxi that was cruising round the square. And then I leaned back in its dark and shabby interior, stale and stuffy with lingering cigarette smoke and the smell left by impatient, tensed-up human creatures, and I rested at last in peace, secure in the knowledge that I had before me at least half an hour of freedom from decision, of freedom. I looked out on traffic blocks, on police diversions and road repairs, with gratitude rather than with anxiety. The taxi ride was my rest cure. I quoted Stevenson: to travel hopefully is better than to arrive, and amended it to suit myself: to travel, hoping never to arrive. I had to direct the driver the last part of the way; this remote little close was never easy to find.

The house was as pretty and neat as ever, at its best with the front garden alight with tulips and wallflowers.

"Mrs. Harmond!" The stocky little white-haired woman who opened the door lingered long on the "ar" as she always used to do.

"Hullo, Elsa. Are they at home?"

It was like a dream; or perhaps it was the other that was the nightmare. After all, it was only two years ago that I had visited them with Robert, on just such a glowing afternoon in May, and they had sat him on the back lawn where he could feel the richness of the colour, smell the sweetness, listen to the constant gentle twittering and humming of birds and insects. I had sat beside him then, with my eyes closed, as I so often did, allowing my other senses to take control, that I might the more match my own experience with his.

They were in the back garden now. Would I go straight through?

"You're looking very well, Elsa," I said.

She smiled and shrugged. "Old, old. One becomes old."

I found myself glancing around in order to help Robert over the step as I walked through the conservatory.

They were both lying back in long garden chairs, their heads in the shade, mouths slightly open, eyes shut, hands falling limply. Two very old people, childless, grown alike in many, many years of loving companionship. Even thus

might Robert and myself have lain, one May afternoon forty
years on, had I not . . .

Had I not what? Had I not fallen in love with Estelle, I
suppose. That must have been what I was going to say.

I had to touch them, as well as speak to them before they
realised that there was anyone there.

"Uncle Jimmy."

"What, what, who?" He started and began to pant a little.

I sat down on the grass beside him and spoke soothingly.
Aunt Laura awoke too in fright, and I had to comfort and
reassure them both.

"You should have given us warning, Mary," she said.
"We thought you were in Cornwall. It's a shock to old folks
like us to wake up and see you here. You're looking very
thin, isn't she, James?"

"There never was very much of her. Nothing much for a
man to get hold of." The old man chuckled a little.

"James!" Aunt Laura's sharpness showed a hint of her
early school-teacher days. She looked at him anxiously. Her
mind has kept stronger than his, I thought: she is afraid he
will forget and say something he ought not to say.

I had not meant to talk about it. If I had intended anything
in my desperate taxi ride, it had been simply to seek the
refuge of my own childhood; but there was something in the
old lady's behaviour that told me I should have to speak.
She would not force it, but she would be happier if I did.
She wanted to hear from my own lips that I was not a
murderess.

We drank tea from pale blue porcelain in the cool
drawing-room and I explained what I was doing in London.

"You ought to have come straight to us," they said
reproachfully, but yet I could sense underneath that they
were relieved I had not come.

"I thought you might not want—that you might still
think—that people would talk. Auntie Laura!" I heard my

voice rising in hysteria, "do you know what it is like to have people believing you have murdered your husband?"

"Now, Mary, pull yourself together. You have been acquitted by a British court of law after fair trial and there is no better justice on God's earth, and only an evil mind could believe you guilty."

"Then you don't—you and Uncle Jimmy don't?"

"My dear child."

They exchanged looks, and the old man's eyes were bleary, and he seemed to understand and yet he seemed not to understand.

"You must not go on like that, Mary," his wife said. "You will make yourself ill. You *have* made yourself ill. You should have come straight away after it happened. You could have come to us."

Very reproachful still.

But you didn't ask me, you didn't ask me, sang out my own mind. You wrote with love and sympathy and comfort, but you didn't ask me.

"I was ill," I said. "Very ill after the trial. I didn't want to leave my doctor—nor Professor Barlow. I had to go back home—in spite of everything."

"Since we *are* talking about it," said Aunt Laura, "although I did not intend to do so and thought you would prefer not to—since we are, then please do tell me, Mary, what sort of a young man is this—Dennis? Derek?— Estelle's friend—why should he have been so determined to secure your conviction? James and I have wondered"—and she glanced at the old man who was silent and seemed now quite uncomprehending—"whether he had not a deeper motive. Perhaps he felt that attack was the best method of defence—perhaps he wanted to get *his* accusation in first."

I began to cry, quietly and not hysterically. She was no fool, this old woman. She knew far more about the case than I had expected. They were by no means the other side of the world in a beautiful dream. They were right in the midst of the nightmare too, and there could be no relaxation for me here. Aunt Laura was not entirely sure of my innocence and she wanted to find out. She was offering me a bait, setting a trap. Were I to leap at it and accuse Derek, then I should be given no rest. They would insist that the case be reopened, with him in the dock; at all costs I must clear my own name.

"I don't know why he hated me so," I muttered. "He persecutes me still. If he should find where I now live, all my hopes of peace are gone. He will tell everyone. No one knows about me now—at least, I don't think they do."

The menace of Malcolm was in the quiet and pretty sitting-room; it was my shadow, it was with me always.

"Unless," said my adoptive aunt, "this man Derek truly believed you responsible for the death of his fiancée—of Estelle. That I suppose would give him the motive to force the trial."

"But how could he—how could he think so!" I cried. "Unless it is a sin to be unable to swim! Or a crime that I did not prevent her from going to her father's aid. He can barely swim himself—he made no attempt to stop her or to save her."

"You know, Mary," said the old lady more gently, "I never did quite understand what actually did happen. Would you like to tell me?"

Another baited trap? If so, there was no way out. But why try to escape? It was easy enough; had I not been drilled in the narration day after day by my counsel? Was it not imprinted on my memory?

"We were going for a picnic," I said, "in the cove. You remember the place. You can drive right to the water's edge. It's tarmac but there's no barrier along the seawall— you have to be careful how you park and how you turn the car or else you're over the edge and it's pretty deep and the tides and rocks can be nasty. But it's a beautiful spot and hardly anyone knows it—we nearly always had it to ourselves. I used to let the others get out with the picnic things while I turned the car round ready to drive away. I would get out myself and settle Robert somewhere quite safe out of the way first, of course. But on this day Derek was with us, and he took the picnic things and stood over to the side, and Estelle was guiding Robert, so there was no need for me to get out. I swung round as usual and drove a yard or two forwards. And then reversed." I had to pause and swallow. It was difficult to speak. This was always the bit of the narrative where I broke down; it had done me no harm in court, my counsel said. "I suppose—I may have—perhaps knowing Estelle was there to see to her father—I suppose I may not have been quite so careful as usual—there's always a blind spot reversing—and I—oh, Auntie Laura, Auntie Laura!"

"Go on, Mary."

She was sitting very tense and upright; like the members of the jury.

I covered my face with my hands. "I hit him. I didn't even know—didn't even hear the splash. I didn't even know at first what had happened till Derek yelled. And when I got out I saw Estelle in the water too—she had jumped in and was fighting and fighting—but the tides are terrible there. It was hopeless. Hopeless."

"So neither you nor Derek went to try to save them?"

"We can't swim—what would have been the use?"

"Nor went for help?"

"I drove straight up to the farm at once, of course. It was far too late. It was bound to be."

I sat quietly crying again. It was over once more; I could weep now in relief. For a while there was silence, broken only by the gentle snoring of the old man.

"Mary," said Aunt Laura, "tell me the truth. It will go no further. You have been acquitted by a British court of law. But there is a higher court which will judge you. Tell me the truth. Did you aim to kill your husband?"

"No! No! No!" I was screaming again. "I loved him—loved him! Cannot you see that I am dead myself without him?"

She looked at me searchingly. "Yes. That might be true. And Estelle—you loved her too?"

"Yes, yes!" I cried.

"But not in any—not in any way that was not right? That was all false, wasn't it, Mary?"

"Of course, of course!" I cried again. "It was an accident—oh God, I don't know how—but it was an accident! Why can't they believe me? Thousands are killed by cars every day. No one calls it murder. It was *accident, accident, accident!*"

"Be quiet, Mary, you will disturb your uncle. I am sorry we raised the subject. It is too distressing for you. We will only have to suppose that this young man was so unbalanced by the death of the girl he loved that he made up this tale of your having driven deliberately at your husband. There are such people—weak and vicious and irresponsible."

"That's Derek," I said more quietly.

"And fortunately British justice does not convict on the word of one witness alone—it requires more solid evidence. And the tracks left by car tyres—and the angle of impact—and the bruises on the body—such things are notoriously capable of misinterpretation. Strange things happen in accidents."

I lay back exhausted in the armchair; I scarcely heard the thin, precise old voice.

"We must be grateful that it all ended as it did," she continued after a pause, "and you must learn to live with your experience. You could marry again, Mary."

I shuddered. "No—oh no."

The old man woke with his nervous start and looked at me. His voice was very feeble:

"Mary? It's our little Mary. But where's Robert? Don't let

him wander about alone—not right. You're too thin, Mary—
no good. A man likes something to get hold of—specially
when he's blind—yes, specially when he's blind."

His eyes were very dull and he shook his head again and
again. My tears and my shuddering stopped suddenly and I
was beyond all feeling. Then I got up and leaned over and
kissed him.

"Goodbye, Uncle Jimmy. We have to go now. It's been
nice to see you."

"Robert"—he muttered—"where's Robert?"

"He's in the car," I said. "I won't disturb him. I'll say
goodbye to him for you."

Aunt Laura followed me out of the room.

"I'm sorry," I said to her as we stood in the hall. "I
shouldn't have come."

"Perhaps not." She was holding herself very stiffly, but
her voice shook. "We are both too old. It's a great shock."

I put my arm round her shoulders and kissed her. "I am
sorry," I said again, and then I could find nothing else to
say. We moved out into the front garden in silence. Aunt
Laura stooped to cradle a tulip in her hand, and then she
came slowly to the gate.

"Oh!" she exclaimed. "Have you no car?"

I shook my head.

"What a pity—a crack driver like you!"

I kissed her again and walked with quick steps down the
road.

7

And yet it had done me good. Harrowing and terrible as it had been, the visit had brought me comfort, for it had given me back my past, my past of long ago. I had been called by my own name, been spoken to with kindness by those who knew. I grieved for the shock and distress I had caused, but I could not regret that I had gone. It had eased my sick mind; by restoring me to my true identity it had given me the strength once more to assume my false one.

I travelled home slowly by bus, this time faintly looking forward to the journey's end. My heart quickened as I turned the corner into the square. Very soon, in all likelihood, I should see Judy again. It was days since I had seen her. I noticed, without much interest, that there was a white sports car parked unlawfully just outside the house. But as I drew nearer I saw a familiar sandy head above the steering wheel, motionless, eyes lowered, intent on the mysteries beneath. I stopped still in surprise, a foot away from the ugly long bonnet and the oddly squinting headlights. What on earth was Tom Prescott doing with a brand new Jaguar sports model? Whatever could have induced him to spend all the deposit money for his house and commit himself to hire purchase for years to come?

He looked up and saw me and a welcoming grin spread over his face.

"Hullo, Miss Wentworth. Isn't it super?"

I agreed cautiously. He speaks to me quite naturally, I thought; nothing, then, has been said; I am still safe.

"Cruise at hundred and twenty—easy. I wish I could take it out on the M1," he said wistfully.

Silently I echoed the wish, but aloud I said:

"I don't know much about cars—but this certainly looks very impressive. When did you get it?"

He laughed, stepped out of the driver's seat, and stood lovingly surveying the car for a moment before he replied:

"It isn't mine, you know. Not a hope! It's Malcolm's. He only got it this morning. He's just brought it round to show us. We're going out in a minute."

"Oh." I digested this. There might be possibilities here. It might just be that this new development could be to my advantage. "Where is he?" I asked.

"Malcolm? Upstairs with Judy—trying to persuade her to come. I don't think she will. She's a bit scared of fast driving and anyway it's not comfortable for three."

"Oh well, have a nice time," I said brightly, and I hurried upstairs to my own room, anxious to get there without seeing the others, for it had suddenly occurred to me that to be able to say I had been spending a few days with old family friends would be a convincing piece of background for my personality; but while Tom, absorbed in this gorgeous toy, would not notice that I carried no suitcase, neither Judy nor Malcolm were likely to be so unobservant. I did not think they would have seen me from the window; the balconies effectively obscured the view of the pavement beneath.

I was in luck. I came out of my room a moment later with very much the air of one who has just dumped a suitcase and is going to the bathroom, at the same time as Judy and Malcolm emerged from next door.

"Hullo!" It was they who were surprised, slightly taken aback.

"Hullo, Judy," I said, and nodded and smiled at Malcolm in recognition. "I've just seen Tom. Have a nice ride." I was very brisk and schoolmistress-like, forcing myself to it, forcing myself not to look too closely at Malcolm in search of signs that he knew all my story.

We each stood back to let the others descend the stairs first. Then Judy moved forward, held on to the banisters, and hesitated, looking from me to Malcolm and then back again.

"I—I . . ." she began.

"Go on, sweetie, it's getting late." Malcolm put a hand on her shoulder and gave her a very slight push. Still not looking at him too closely, I received an impression of thick and glossy brown hair, beautiful brown suède, and a very faint and elusive scent. I also received the impression that he was, for the time being at least, paying no attention whatever to me, but was interested simply in showing the Prescotts his new car. It hung in the air, as intangible as the scent, this aura of innocent, normal humanity; it even gave him a slight air of pathos. Nigel Reeves, I thought. A good-looking man—or perhaps not quite a man; not so young as he was; maybe a little lonely; looking forward to the great pleasure of showing off his proud and happy ownership, arousing admiration and envy if he could not arouse love.

A commonplace enough occurrence, harmless, not at all sinister. Let them go and admire; let them go. They were all three of them happy enough in their own way; it was I who was the intruder.

I smiled again. "You'd better hurry—it's getting late."

"Too right," said Malcolm, and he gave Judy another little push.

She shook him off petulantly and stepped back up on the landing.

"I don't want to go, Malcolm. I don't like fast driving, and now Miss Wentworth's back, I want to talk to her."

She looked at me appealingly. She is genuinely scared, I thought, but at the same time I knew she was not unaware of making mischief, and above all my reasoning was an idiotic, blazing triumph: she wants me, she likes me, she loves me—and mingled with that triumph was alarm. The moment of commonplace human feeling was over; the danger lights were flashing. I could feel those cold and startling blue eyes of Malcolm's upon me and it cost me a tremendous effort not to look at him and not to flinch.

"I'm sorry, Judy," I said firmly. "I'm afraid I'm not free. I've just this moment got back from visiting some old friends—I stayed longer than I meant to and I've a great deal of work to catch up with from the last few days. So please excuse me this evening."

I manœuvred past her, ran hastily down to the landing, and disappeared into the bathroom. From behind the locked door I heard quick steps on the stairs, an impatient exclamation from Malcolm, and then a door slammed above. A moment later a horn sounded loudly and there was the roar of a powerful motor. I waited in the bathroom until I judged that all was clear, and then I returned to my room. The unwashed coffee cups stood on the table; the open suitcase was eloquent of my desperate indecision of the morning, which I now found difficult to recall, so many days and years of experience seemed to have elapsed between that time and this. I was still afraid, still convinced—in spite of that odd little moment of illusion on the landing—that Malcolm knew my secret and wished me ill; but the malaise that had overcome me with the shock of the accident on the zebra crossing seemed at last to have worked itself out and I could reason and plan and act again.

I tidied up the room—never, in my right mind, would I have left it looking so messy—drew out my briefcase and tried to settle myself down to checking through my tran-

scriptions of the previous week. I would like to send a
parcel off to Professor Barlow the following Monday; it
would be an excuse to write to him, and writing my
customary brief little covering note was always of comfort
to me, a reassurance of my own identity. Beyond these little
exchanges I would not presume. The old man had known
me only as Robert's wife, the wife of the man with whom
he had played a weekly game of chess for many years, his
only meeting with human beings apart from the faithful
couple who looked after him. He had tolerated me only as
a necessary means for transporting Robert; I had been
permitted a few words on bringing Robert there, a few more
when I came to fetch him. And then he had not only lost his
only friend, but had been dragged through everything that
his brilliant and fearful intellect held most horrible in order
to save the life of that friend's widow. I did not know the
cause of his intense shrinking from human contact, but I
could see and understand that for him to bear the gaze of the
public and the enquiries of the law was the equivalent of the
normal man's nightmare of fleeing, naked, from some
unknown terror in a crowded street.

At least I was being of some small use to him now; not
only in carrying out my specific commission, but in
performing many little services in connection with his
writing—trivial enough matters for the usual publicity-
minded scholar of today, with his armoury of agents and
secretaries and other auxiliaries, but an intolerable burden
on a man like Professor Barlow. I could send him the latest
batch of letters and also report on the telephone call I had
made to his publishers. And perhaps I might also venture to
comment on the performance of *Rosenkavalier* that I had
treated myself to at Covent Garden, and I had the privilege
of signing myself simply by my Christian name.

"Mary," he had said to me before I left, "I do not think
it wise to call yourself by a false name. You will not escape
it that way."

How right he had been! Would I not have done better to come in my own name, with my own history? To look up all my former acquaintances, brave it out at once? I had told him I could not do it. "I am not so much unlike you in this respect," I had said to him, and he had been unable to find an answer.

I stared at my own small and taut handwriting—intense emotion held precariously under rigid control, a graphologist had once said of it—and could not make sense of what I had written. These letters of an early Victorian Member of Parliament were eloquent and interesting but had at the moment no power to grip me. I was intensely conscious, as I sat in the one armchair and glanced every now and then out of the window, of the human being in the adjoining room, the other side of the thin partition. What had she done after I had so publicly snubbed her? Was she offended? How would she show it? What was she doing now?

I could hear no sound. I put down my papers and shut my eyes, to concentrate the more keenly. Only the intermittent traffic and occasional voice from the street; the radio—a string quartet—from Dennis and Harry's flat, and the quick and muffled step on the staircase of one of the Indians. The sound of water running from the bathroom—this so faint that I was not normally aware of it at all. And then, in an unusually quiet patch, another sound, very faint and indeterminate, something between a sniff and a cough. I listened, my eyelids screwed up, every muscle tense. It came again, but I could not tell from where.

Amidst all the normal evening sounds of a square in Bloomsbury it seemed to me that someone was crying. It need not necessarily be Judy. It could be Liz, from above, in one of her frequent fits of uncontrolled fury or frustration or despair. It could be from the street—some lovers' tiff just under my balcony: it could be from next door. It could be from somebody's television set that only today, with my abnormally alert hearing, was audible to me.

And yet I was sure it was Judy and that she was crying because I had rejected her. Silly little girl, I said to myself; just because she looks so angelic she need not think everyone is constantly at her beck and call. She will have to learn. And at the thought of Judy having to learn, having to be patient and wretched, aching for a kind word, wondering what she had done wrong, my heart quickened once again with excitement and triumph. What power was in my tongue! The power to wound, to raise hopes and then dash them. I will have you begging for kindness and pity, yes you, my beauty, who think you can rule all you survey, who believe me to be so helplessly in your toils.

I drifted into day-dreaming—the sort of dreaming that was second nature with me. Judy—Estelle—or sometimes it was the pretty little dark English mistress from my old school—but always we were in a world of our own, caught up out of time and space into an eternity of intense emotion, where there was no reality except the strength of this feeling, which never wavered.

It grew dark. It was just such a clear and showery evening as that when I had first arrived in the square. I loved the view. It had grown into myself. Green grass among the concrete, flowers at the heart—how poignant and life-giving is a city garden. A car drew up under my balcony and there were loud and cheerful voices. Hastily I drew the curtains, pulled out my portable typewriter, and sat down and poked jerkily at the space bar. I had said I was working; it must sound as if I were. I should have thought of it before. I began to copy my own transcripts, though I did not normally trouble to do so. It would look more convincing if someone were to come in. I pressed the keys and my eyes darted back and forth; but I was listening for the footsteps on the stairs, the sound of the opening door, the first greetings which would tell me whether indeed she had been crying there alone, or whether it was my own imaginings.

The steps came—Tom usually took them two at a time,

Malcolm was more sedate. The door closed. In the pauses of my typing I heard an occasional sound from next door. I could hardly sit still. It became intolerable to be shut out, kept in ignorance like this. Judy, what are you doing, what are you feeling? Do you care at all, do you care? Of course she did not care. They were all three laughing at me, poor old thing, typing away. Where was the sobbing? I had been wrong all along; she had been out with them too; they had all come in together; it was something totally different that I had heard.

My own eyes began to fill. I hit the keys at random and not until a few seconds after it had sounded did I realise that there had been a knock on the door. I glanced in the mirror as I rose and, with the deep protective instinct of the hunted and the hiding, I also glanced briefly about the room. All was in order; my story of the visit to friends would hold.

He stood there, tall and posed and gorgeous, and I could not understand why it was not Judy who had come.

"I'm very sorry to disturb you, Miss Wentworth. Please forgive the intrusion."

I stepped back and he followed me into the room.

"What's the matter?" I hoped I sounded brusque. The typewriter and the papers lying beside it gave me confidence.

"It's Judy." He gave a little deprecatory smile and a shrug. "As you have no doubt observed, she rules us all—her wish is law."

He looked at me apologetically, but I knew that the ice-blue eyes had seen the typewriter and the pages of writing and everything else in the room.

"What's the matter with her?" I asked. Fear and hope; alarm and joy—they were all there together.

He glanced down at the table, picked up a sheet of my writing and began to read it, as he went on in pretended embarrassment: "She thinks she has somehow offended you and appears to be inconsolable."

"Nonsense."

"Ah yes, to you and me perhaps. But to the victim of the Schwärmerei only too real." He looked full at me now and smiled again.

Dorian Grey, I thought, suddenly recalling vividly that story that had always held a peculiar horror for me. Beautiful, spotless, faultless exterior; and rotten inside, evil, evil, evil.

"But really, Mr. . . ." I expostulated. "But really. . . ." It was too absurd that I still did not know his name. "Really this is quite ridiculous. I am sorry if Judy is upset, but I don't see what I have got to do with it."

I sat down at the chair where I had been typing. Let me get on with my work and don't worry me, the action was meant to say to him, but my mind was a tumult. I was right: Judy cares—she's in love with me! Judy, angelic, heavenly Judy!

"You want to work," he said, though we both knew this was not true, "and I assure you I have come very reluctantly."

I sighed in resignation. "What do you want me to do?"

"If you could spare a moment—just to reassure her." He paused and looked down once again at my sheets of writing. "Interesting stuff, and what a rare legibility of hand," he went on in a different tone of voice, implying that we were two serious people, interested more in scholarship than in the childish nonsense of Judy's fancies. I was not taken in; it was the latter that was dominating both our minds.

"Do you always type it all out?" he asked.

"Only when the mood takes me," I said lightly enough, but the danger signals were flashing—take care, it's coming near.

"Over-conscientious, as so many academic women are," he said in a voice so good-natured that it softened the familiar gibe. "What's Parry Barlow really like?—to talk to, I mean."

Clever, oh, clever! A trap held by a hairspring, set with casual ease.

"Professor Barlow," I repeated. "I don't know. I've never met him."

"Oh no, of course. I forgot."

I took the page out of the typewriter and began to put the machine away. I had to do something to conceal the shaking of my hands. "I don't suppose I'll be doing any more work tonight," I said.

"Good of you to come," he remarked, and turned away, ostensibly to look at the few books I had set out on a rack. It's just as I thought, I told myself grimly; to the edge, and then rescue, and then again. It will be like this again and again. The Parry Barlow line. This is my weakest defence. That had been news indeed a year ago—Scholar Recluse in Witness Box—that had drawn the eye more than the wretched creature in the dock; although of course my parents' names, even years after their deaths, were still worth quoting. As for Robert, he had not had much news value in himself. A rich man indeed, but not the only well-off business man who had retired early to live in the country.

All this went through my mind as I clicked the lock of the typewriter case and placed it on the floor, and I was also mentally picturing the row of books at which Malcolm was looking. A few recent novels in paperback, a dictionary, a London street plan, a bedside anthology, a widely read popular history of nineteenth century England. My mind went no further, unless I had placed my current library books on the shelf.

"Nice part of the world, Cornwall," said Malcolm in the most casual of tones, and then it hit me, the cold, sick, horrified recollection that among a few guidebooks was a little chatty anthology about Cornwall, in an "English Counties" series, and that somewhere between its pages there was slipped a photograph of my home, cut from a magazine about five years ago, when it had been featured in a series dealing with the conversion of old houses. It was with the utmost difficulty that I restrained myself from flinging myself at him and pulling the book away.

"Yes, indeed." I was noncommittal. My mind was swarming with explanations. It was a library book; it was borrowed from a friend; I was all astonishment—didn't know how it had got there—must have picked it up by mistake when I left my aunt's cottage in Cornwall after she died. But of course he made no direct mention of it; I should have learnt by now that that was not his way.

"I wouldn't mind picking up an old cottage and tarting it up for myself one day," he went on in the same offhand manner.

Could it possibly be coincidence? Had he really not seen the cutting?"

"Neither would I," I said, and then I could drag out the business of putting the typewriter away no longer, and was obliged to look up. "I'm just running down to the landing," I said, "and then I'll be with you."

It was a clear dismissal; he could hardly linger on in my room during the few minutes I was gone. Nor did he; his manners were impeccable.

"It's very good of you," he said warmly. "Our friend Judy can be more than a little tiresome at times—as you will surely have discovered. But you will have to join with the rest of us in spoiling her—who could help it?"

He smiled at me once more—a true Nigel Reeves smile, and left the room.

My own toothy grin came unstuck with difficulty. I ran to the book-rack the moment the Yale lock had clicked behind him. The Cornwall book was there, right at the end. I opened it, and the pages fell apart near the beginning, opposite a rather poor photograph of Land's End. They say that if you pick up a book that has just been shut, the leaves will fall open again at the same place. Was this all he had

seen? Had he in fact touched the book at all? Was it
conceivable that he had not even seen it, that the remark
about Cornwall was simply a following up of the Parry
Barlow line? I opened and closed the book twice more.
There was no sign of the magazine cutting. I flicked through
the leaves, my panic rising. Was it there at all? Had it ever
been there? Had I imagined it? Had he found it and
pocketed it? How could I possibly have overlooked such a
vital clue to my identity? How could sentiment so have
overpowered reason?

And yet until this moment I had completely forgotten that
the cutting was there, had indeed temporarily even forgotten
the book; and since my present acquaintance knew in any
case that I had spent some time in Cornwall before coming
to London, the presence of such a widely read little
guide-book could scarcely arouse comment. It had not, after
all, been much of a risk to take.

Apart from the magazine cutting.

I opened the little book and shook it violently. A slip of
paper fell to the floor. I snatched it up and was instantly in
despair because I would now never know from which page
it had fallen. As if that would have helped, cold reason told
me; since you have no recollection of where and when you
slipped it in you could not have told whether it had been
moved. And in any case he would have put it back in the
same place.

But perhaps he had not seen it. He could only have held
the book, if at all, for a second or two. Of course he had not
seen it. The very intensity of the wish carried conviction
with it. I replaced the book and held the cutting crumpled up
in my hand. I must destroy it instantly. I looked around the
room. No fireplace. And in any case I must not leave a
tell-tale smell or tell-tale ashes.

Of course. I had said I wanted to go down to the
bathroom, which included the W.C. Moving once more as
an automaton, I picked up my cigarette lighter and ran

down the stairs. The little slip of newsprint in my hand was like a living, burning thing, venomous and threatening. I held it to the flame, over the lavatory pan. It must be destroyed, utterly, absolutely; I could not make sure enough. It burnt with difficulty—it must have become damp in my sweating hand. It blackened, became crisp and fragile, and at length it fell into the water. It scorched my fingers, and I let fall the last square inch of paper. I could see it as it fell; it was the margin, with scarcely a black print mark on it. The pan seemed full of burnt fragments. I looked on them with something of relief, something of nostalgia. And then I pulled the old-fashioned chain, and as the water swirled and the last scrap disappeared from view I felt as if I had flushed my whole life away.

But it was Robert who had drowned, and Estelle with him.

I was bewildered. I looked around at the big old bath tub with the green stain under the tap, and at the dirty cream walls and the torn brown lino. And then I looked once more in the pan. The water was still and clear. It was all gone; all safely gone, never to be recovered. I was safe, safe, safe for ever. And then up in front of my eyes I saw the black fragments reappear, scatter themselves round the brown-veined old enamel, crackle on the water. I gave a little cry, and pulled the chain again. And then I think I lost consciousness for a second, because I swayed against the wall, and when I was sound and upright again my mind was clear, and I knew that the paper was indeed destroyed beyond recall, and only the intensity of my fear had brought up its image to my mind. I slid back the bolt on the door and returned slowly to my room. The panic receded. It ebbed and flowed like the tide; I should be growing accustomed to it by now. I washed my hands and combed my hair and made up my face afresh. I was left with the aftermath, the exhaustion, the heaviness of total non-feeling, non-caring.

8

I went next door, and with great effort I dredged up from a feeling past the reason for my presence, the knowledge that I was supposed to be reassuring Judy for my apparent snubbing of her.

She was soon convinced, or appeared to be. My own genuine unawareness commanded belief.

"But my dear child," I chided her, "you really must not take a temporary inability to fit in with your plans as a mortal insult. Good heavens, social intercourse would become utterly impossible if one could never refuse an invitation or put off an engagement without producing a crisis of this sort!"

"That's just what I told her," said Tom. "Honestly, Judy, you are hopeless, and it's jolly lucky it's someone as understanding as Miss Wentworth this time."

This time? The implication penetrated even my dullness. I had been right, then, in my estimate of her. This sort of complicated build-up of relationships with other people was not something new, even in Judy's short married life.

"Poor Tom," I said laughing. "So you've been through all this before?"

He related an instance. A somewhat sophisticated, older colleague of Judy's whom they had seen a lot of a few

months ago. It was nothing but "have I offended Mrs.
Cambridge?" . . . "d'you think we bored her?" . . .
"d'you think I shouldn't have suggested that film?"—and
so on ad infinitum.

I studied him as he spoke. He appeared perfectly cheerful
and unresentful. An ordinary young husband speaking of
his wife with affectionate mockery to friends who knew and
cared for them both. He might not be particularly bright, but
in some respects he certainly knew his Judy. She bossed
him about but she depended on him too. I looked at Judy.
She was curled up in an armchair; her hair was in even
greater disarray than usual, and I thought her eyes looked
slightly red. But she gave a little sly, conscious smile as
Tom spoke, and glanced first at Malcolm and then at me.
Tom is only being allowed to go on like this because she
thinks it makes her appear interesting, I thought. He will
not often get the chance to hold forth—Malcolm and Judy
will carry most of the conversation between them.
And Malcolm will shut him up now when he has had
enough; Malcolm knows very well how to manage them
both, Malcolm knows it all. I watched him lean back in his
chair in apparent tolerance mingled with faint disdain. What
a pity it is that we are deadly enemies, my thoughts ran on;
we have a lot in common, our minds work the same way. If
we were friends, and if I had not a desperate secret to hide,
why, how we could enjoy analysing Judy together, capping
each other's insights with an ever-lengthening spiral of
ingenious suppositions!

And not Judy's character alone, but also any other mutual
acquaintance, any public figure even, could be thus happily
and minutely dissected. For fascinating and stimulating
conversations, for really good company, there is nothing to
beat an intelligent homosexual, I thought. And if he doesn't
look like one, and is very good-looking, why, what a
satisfying sexless friendship could develop and how pleasant to be regarded with envy by other women! Within

limits, of course, because naturally there would be no real confidence and trust; it would be a thing of the mind and the spoken word alone, and one would have to accept that there would be backbiting and bitchiness. All the same, it was an attractive picture to one so starved of intellectual company, and as I sat listening to the "You did," "I didn't" conversation that had arisen between Tom and Judy as a result of his narration of her social gaffes, it seemed more desirable than ever.

I caught Malcolm's eye. He winked. A large, good-natured, friendly wink. I smiled back. The other two were oblivious.

"Children," said Malcolm, getting up and standing over them. "You are boring Miss Wentworth—you are boring me. Cease this tedious squabbling and attend to the needs of your guests. Why do we not have coffee?"

Judy sprang up, flustered and apologetic, and busied herself in the little kitchen alcove. I turned to Tom:

"Where did you try out the car?"

Anything to put the conversation on to a harmless, impersonal level. My recent thoughts had stirred me out of my exhaustion. Malcolm was my deadly enemy. Never must I forget it. His apparent friendliness, his inviting me to join with him in laughing at the others, this was no goodwill but was part of the whole vicious scheme. A baited trap to draw the victim even further in. It was meant to catch me off my guard, to expose my weakness. "You've not been gone long enough to get beyond the speed limit," I added.

Tom merely laughed.

"Well," drawled Malcolm, "I reckon we did ninety—or was it more?—along the North Circular, didn't we, Tom?"

"Good Lord," I cried, "you'll be run in!"

"We nearly were."

There was a little cry of horror from the kitchen corner where Judy was setting out the coffee cups. "I *do* wish you wouldn't drive so fast, Tom!" she called out.

"Surely such a car is not very practical in London," I said quickly, hoping to forestall another argument between Tom and Judy. "I realise that it must be great fun to drive—but will you get much use out of it?"

This time it was with Tom that Malcolm exchanged looks of complete understanding.

"Have you never yearned to possess something entirely impractical and senseless?"

It seemed a harmless enough question, but I was becoming uneasy at the personal twist that the conversation was taking. "Well, yes, I suppose so," I said reluctantly.

Malcolm shrugged. "Well, then."

It was the same friendly tone as before, but this time it aroused once more the cold little swell of fear.

"I suppose I am unsympathetic because my extravagance does not lie in that direction," I said as lightly as I could.

"Oh really? I'd have put you down as a good driver. Rallies maybe. Steady nerves, self-control, ready to cope with anything."

"I'd have said so too," said Tom, and they both looked at me.

I tried to laugh it away. "What a reputation to have acquired on so slight an acquaintance! No, I've never driven in a rally, and I am not a good driver, though I confess I quite enjoy the sort of leisurely pootling around that so infuriates you sports car owners."

"Would you like to try the sports car for a change?" asked Malcolm.

"No! Not on your life," I cried, and the shudder I gave was by no means all assumed. "I'd be scared stiff."

I was rescued by Judy emerging from the alcove with a tray. Her silly little shift dress was crumpled and showed at the hem the greyish line of a once-white nylon slip, and her mascara was smudgy and there was a petulant tilt to the nose and to the perfect lips. For one extraordinary second I saw right through to her commonplace and dishonest little soul; saw her as sluttish, stupid, and untrustworthy; saw her as I would have seen her had she been a plain girl with dull hair and eyes and a prim unyielding mouth. As I had seen straight through to the heart of the girl in the Manuscript Room.

In that second my chains were cut and I was set free and I exulted that I could go away, save what little life and future there might remain for me, and escape this torment of uncertainty, this horror of exposure. Escape from Malcolm.

But it lasted only the second. Judy came towards me and handed me my cup with great care. It was as if it were a peace offering. "I made it strong especially for you," she said. "I do hope it's all right."

It wasn't. There were pieces of boiled milk skin floating unattractively on the muddy liquid. But I took it with a great show of being touched, and indeed I was moved nearly to tears, maudlin with self-pity. Fancy someone still caring enough about me to consult my taste, I said to myself, and I smiled back and thanked her, and she knew she had me once again at her mercy.

And then Malcolm cried out in disgust: "My God! Why do I bother with you two! Nothing but silly arguments and undrinkable coffee. It's too much. Really it's too much." And he sounded perfectly genuine, and it was so exactly what I felt myself that I suddenly liked him again, and I saw him as a lonely, pitiful creature, unhappy for all his gifts and his posturing, fascinated by Judy's beauty, desperately seeking in the friendship of this young couple to ward off his own horror of beauty fading, faculties failing, of solitary, unwanted old age.

Tom laughed happily and said "Poor old Malcolm," and I thought, You hero-worshipping schoolboy, you, you'll never be anything else if you live to be a hundred; and then Judy, catching sight of herself in the mirror, put her hands to her hair and gave a squawk of horror that turned into her rather harsh laugh, and then it seemed that they were

suddenly all three very deferential and considerate and kind
to me, worrying that I was too hot or too cold or not
comfortable, asking my opinion on the news of the day and
Tom's exams and Judy's colleagues and Malcolm's latest
article, and heaven knows what else. And I was totally
exhausted and wanted only to go to my room and sleep.

But I kept my eyes open somehow and made some sort of
reply, until at last Judy got up and stood over me in a
proprietorial manner and said accusingly:

"I believe you've got migraine again. She gets awful
migraines, you know. Tom. I'm going to see you to bed.
You ought to have told us before." And she hustled me from
the room.

My only thought, after at last she had gone, leaving an
indefinable sense of disorder behind her in my tidy room,
was that Malcolm had engineered the whole evening so that
he could get into my room and see my books and find that
newspaper cutting.

But how did he know it was there, I asked myself, as if
it were only a few minutes later, although in fact it was
showing nearly dawn and I had been asleep for hours. I lay
and looked at the greyish slit between the long curtains. I
always pulled them an inch apart last thing at night.
Malcolm did not know it was there, came the answer, but he
suspected that he might find something if only he could get
into the room. And he *had* found something. Or hadn't he?
How could I ever tell whether he had seen the magazine
cutting or not? At any rate there was no danger of his
finding it now; it was destroyed utterly, consumed by fire,
dissolved in water. It was gone.

And then such a glaring, obvious flaw in my reasoning
hit me that I sat up in bed and gasped. How did I know it
was gone? I had destroyed a piece of newsprint, true; but I
had not looked at it. I had snatched it up and assumed it was
the one. How did I know—how could I ever know—that it
was the right one, that it was not just a harmless little

extract, a few amateurish lines of poetry that I might one day have taken the fancy to cut out and slip into the anthology? I did that sort of thing from time to time, and then forgot about it. I had seen nothing clearly but the margin of the paper I had destroyed; it might have been anything.

Then where, then where was the picture of the house? Had he got it? Or was it still there in the book?

I clicked on the bedside lamp and, shivering, walked over to the bookshelf. I drew out the Cornwall anthology and took it back with me to bed. No panic now; this was too important; I must control myself and search really carefully, make quite, quite sure. Better make some tea first, and light a cigarette; that would steady my nerves for the vital task. I did this, and then ten minutes later was back in bed again, turning over the pages one by one, running my thumbnail down the edges to make sure there were no two stuck together, poking my fingers deep into the binding so that it almost split apart. Three times I did this; slowly, deliberately, with infinite self-control I went thus through the whole volume until at last it looked ragged and worn as if it had been thrown about for years in secondhand book-sellers' shops.

There was nothing there. I had destroyed the evidence. Or had there been two cuttings and had Malcolm taken the fatal one? I was still stiff with self-control, control over the impulse to run down to the bathroom and try to conjure up the blackened fragments again so that I could learn from them the truth and set my mind at rest.

I scolded myself, aloud, in a whisper: "Mary, if you don't take a firm grip now, you really will go mad. Yes, mad, mad, mad." The short clipped little word became meaningless as I repeated it again and again. If only there were something I could *do*, my mind cried out. Of course you can do something, came the other voice; you can destroy the book.

Poor mangled little book. It lay on the orange candlewick bedspread that I had bought to give some gaiety to my home. Poor little book. It had done no harm. But it would have to go. How to get rid of it. That was not so easy as the cutting. It would take a little thought and ingenuity. It was something to plan for, something to aim towards. I felt a little better as I lay in bed watching the slit between the curtains grow lighter, and making my plans for getting rid of the little book.

9

It is not so easy, though, to dispose of two pieces of cardboard and a hundred leaves of paper when you live in one room in the heart of London. If I used the previous method it might block up the drains; and besides, it would be a long-drawn-out business that my nerves could not bear. I might drop it over Waterloo Bridge, but no doubt some officious creature would notice and would come up and commiserate with me over the mishap. I could not stand that either. It was not easy, but I enjoyed setting my mind to the problem. It gave a direction to my thoughts, made me feel stronger and less afraid.

I slipped the book into my handbag and carried it with me when I went to the bathroom, and later on when I went to pay the rent. I always rather dreaded going down to the basement, and this was the second time in the week that I had been there. Mrs. Willows was very fond of herrings, which she cooked in stale fat and ate at all hours. They combined with the smell of unswept rooms in a damp basement to produce at times a nauseating stench about which all the tenants complained but never took any action, aside from some half-hearted spraying of aerosols by Judy. "She's only a poor old thing," was the general comment, "you can't hurt her feelings."

This Friday morning it was worse than ever, and apparently even the old woman herself had noticed it, because both the front door into the area and the back door into the yard were open, presumably in an attempt to let in some air. Mrs. Willows came in from the yard, clinging to the door frame for support, her faded floral dress nearly dipping to the ground, concealing the crooked limb. She was panting and her face was blotchy and shining with sweat. It was warm for the time of year and the sun was at this hour slanting direct into the yard. I was revolted and yet I could not stop myself from going forward to her aid, and as she leaned on my arm I caught a glimpse of the back yard, squalid and filthy, and an idea stirred within me.

We moved into the front room where she received the rents. It was full of crumbling Victorian furniture and dirty draperies. She took an ancient cashbox out from the cupboard and struggled with the lock. Of all the sloppy ways to do business, I thought; and indeed it was astonishing that the money was never stolen before the company's man came round to collect it.

"You don't look very well," I said as I handed over my notes. "Is there anything I can do?"

I was genuinely sorry for her, this scrap of human wreckage, dragging out her last few years in this cheerless place. She had a widowed daughter-in-law whom she did not like; apart from this I knew little about her. Perhaps she had once been happy and prosperous like myself; perhaps her story was not unlike my own. Her voice was cultured and hinted at a happier past.

To my horror she began to cry. "I ought not to tell you. Mr. Fenton would be angry with me. But I can't manage. I can't, I can't."

"What can't you manage?"

"It's the rubbish men." She dabbed at her face. "They're no help at all, you see. I can't carry the bins through, and I can't get them to do it, but Mr. Fenton says they must, or else they must collect it from the back, and they won't do that either. They're waiting for a tip but I've nothing to give them and he won't give me anything for them. I'm sorry, Miss Wentworth. I shouldn't be telling you all this."

I let her cry a little and murmured a few kind phrases. I could well spare some sympathy, for she had shown me the way.

"What day do they come?" I asked.

"This morning. Any time now."

"Well, don't you worry any more, Mrs. Willows. I'm going to see to it for you. But you mustn't tell Mr. Fenton or anyone else in the house, please. Will you promise me that?"

She nodded. "I'm not a one for gossip. You know that."

It was quite true. Only very occasionally did she lapse into reminiscences, and I myself seemed to be the chief recipient of these.

"All right," I said. "Here's thirty shillings. You are to give it to them and make sure that they clear every scrap of rubbish away. You can tell them the tenants have clubbed together and collected it because they are sick of the mess, and if you can manage it, you can hint that if they do their job properly there may be more to come. I don't want to talk myself, but I'll hang around here and make quite sure they do take it." I cut short her thanks. "Now where are these bins? And you said something about collecting at the back. Can they get round there? And wouldn't it be easier?"

She began to pull herself up from the chair.

"No, don't trouble," I said. "I'll look myself. You don't mind, do you?"

"It's not very nice, Miss Wentworth. You see I can't get up the stairs to collect it, and some of them take it out themselves and drop it anyhow, and some of them leave it in newspaper on my stairs here, and being as I am . . ."

"Yes, yes, I know." I was impatient to be moving. "You wait here. I shan't be long."

I was among those who left it on the stairs wrapped up in newspaper, if I did not take it to a public refuse tin to drop in on my way to work, and I had never been into the back yard. It was fly-ridden and utterly horrible. Half a dozen bent and rusty bins were brimming over on to the paving stones, which were inches deep in newspapers and cigarette ends, vegetable peelings and fishbones, tea-leaves, tins and packages, all sodden with rain, picked over by stray cats. Had it been human excrement it could hardly have been more revolting. I shut my eyes and saw the vision of Judy that was always with me: the flower on the dunghill. Good God, it was a miracle that we were not all down with cholera! And yet shot through my disgust was a thread of martyred pleasure: how I do suffer for you, Judy, even this!

I held my nose and stepped around the bins. Beyond them was a door in the wall and it was open. So that was where the builder's yard led to, the cobbled entrance under the archway that I passed by every day when I turned left out of the square. There was an old bath tub and a sink lying in the roadway, together with some planks, some pieces of iron, and an old-fashioned bedstead, but no sign of human life. The broad wooden gates looked as if they opened on to a warehouse, but it seemed to be little used. A Council refuse van might well find difficulty in negotiating the archway, but an active middle-aged woman could come and go with ease.

I was pleased with my discovery. It had never occurred to me that there might be another entrance to the house, and I found it reassuring. An occasion might arise when it would be useful to escape unseen. The protruding roof of the back of the basement flat obscured the view from the bathroom window, and as for the rest of the house, surely only odd creatures like Liz would be interested in the jumble of roofs and chimneys, and she had already done her painting of them.

I shut the door and returned to the rubbish bins. There was a gaudy cereal carton lying on top of one of them. I took the book from my bag, keeping my back to the house so that any prying eyes could see only that I leant over the bin, slipped it into the cereal packet, filled it up with paper bags and cabbage leaves, and replaced it on top where it showed up clearly. There remained only to wait, and this was a tedious business, sitting with Mrs. Willows in the foetid atmosphere of her living-room, refusing her offers of tea. Her gratitude began to bore me, but it was preferable to the sequel, which was a polite enquiry into my own life and background. I told the usual tale, and fortunately she soon gave up. I don't think she was very interested. She was too beaten down by pain and despair to have much curiosity about other people. We ceased speaking, and there was an odd little bond of sympathy between us.

A clatter of metal and the heavy whirr of a motor told us of the arrival of the dustmen. Mrs. Willows played her part with some spirit, while I stood in the living-room doorway. The bright-coloured carton was carried past. I moved to the window to look up and see it tipped with a shower of tins and paper into the maw of the machine. The men moved on. It was all over. I went out into the yard and saw that they had done a fair job, and that only a thin slime remained in the bins and on the ground. All the substantial stuff had gone, and there were no blackened fragments to rise up and torment me this time. I felt a great upwelling of relief, as if I had cast out a devil. Mrs. Willows was tearful in her thanks, and I felt too the little glow that comes from doing good.

I set off for work with a brisk and purposeful step. The new sense of confidence stayed with me all day, and when the hour came for the Manuscript Room to shut, I found that I did not want to go quietly home, but wanted company and intelligent conversation.

"Are you free this evening?" I asked the girl at the desk, whose name I had learned was Alice. "Would you care to come round to my place and have a light meal and a chat?"

She accepted willingly. It was rather pleasant to stroll along the street with a companion by my side. And I was delighted when the Prescotts emerged from their room at the very moment that I was bringing Alice up the stairs into mine, for although I made no introduction it was obvious that she was my guest. It killed two birds at once. First, it went far to establishing my bona fides, for a mysterious woman who never has a visitor, even if her home is only a room in a lodging house and entertaining is difficult, is surely suspect. Second, it made Judy jealous. This latter became obvious to me the next day, and I took considerable satisfaction in parrying Judy's enquiries, refusing to gratify her curiosity.

"She's in the same line as myself" was all that I would say. "We like to compare notes now and then."

The implication was of a long-standing friendship, an intellectual companionship to which Judy could never aspire, and this too served a dual purpose. Judy sulked all the week-end, and I enjoyed it greatly.

But reaction had to come. A few evenings later I overheard her greeting Malcolm with particular fondness, and my punishing of her seemed a poor, cold, worthless pleasure. I sat by my window and was overcome with a great sense of loss, of total desolation. I even regretted having destroyed the book. It was as if I had taken a yet greater stride away from all that remained of my former self. I was drifting helplessly, a prey to irrational terrors. I sat on and on after darkness fell; the silly noise from next door went on hour after hour, and nobody asked me in.

In the morning Alice remarked that I was looking tired. She began to fuss me. Not unlike Judy, only she was much more efficient at it. I had little patience with her this morning and it was all I could do to make the polite response that was her due. She wanted to come back with me after work to see that I got a good meal, and I had the greatest difficulty in shaking her off. I could only get away by promising to visit her and her mother the following week-end at their house in a south London suburb. It was stupid of me to have opened up this relationship, for there would be no escaping her now so long as I was working in the Manuscript Room, and I still had a good couple of weeks' more transcribing to do there.

Two weeks. Professor Barlow had suggested various jobs I could carry out for him after that, but I was not absolutely committed to them. I had become so obsessed with the struggle to avoid discovery that I had hardly realised that my work was approaching its end. I could summon up no interest in further commissions; I could form no conception of how things would be at the end of another two weeks. It seemed impossible that the time would ever come. Long before that there would be—there must be—a crisis. I could no longer live in this atmosphere of suspicion and suspense, with this terrible threat of exposure hanging over my head.

I began to think that Malcolm had already told all he knew. Judy and I were friends once more, but sometimes it seemed to me that she looked at me in horror and disgust, and that she was keeping my secret only to await the moment when my exposure would be the most torturing and humiliating to myself. And then later on I would realise that this was my own imagining; she would smile at me so enchantingly, be so touchingly concerned for my welfare, that, knowing her to be no actress, to be incapable, for all her deceit, of playing this sort of part, I realised that, so far as she was concerned at any rate, my past was unknown.

And unknown it must remain. Destroyed, irrecoverable, just as the little book was destroyed beyond recovery. The book had shown me the way. It held my secret, and I had got rid of it. Malcolm held my secret too; I must get rid of him.

I thought again of trying to buy him off. It was indeed surprising that he had not yet approached me for blackmail money; his car had cost a vast sum, he must surely be in need of cash. I would go to him, weary, resigned, and say: "All right. You win. How much do you want?"

We could come to a regular arrangement; we might even become quite friendly over it; it would be a relief to talk to someone about my past—to be myself for a while—even if that someone were my blackmailer. I wondered how much he would ask for, and began vaguely to plan which securities I would sell in order to raise the money. There might be a little difficulty here. I had kept my bank account at home, and made only a temporary arrangement to cash cheques at the London branch. It was a big West End branch, with much coming and going of clients, and in any case I had arranged to sign cheques in my maiden name after my acquittal. I doubted very much whether anyone at the branch had the least suspicion of who I was. But if I were to withdraw large amounts of cash, that would immediately draw attention to me. And if I were to sell securities and draw out large cheques for Malcolm on my Cornish account, well, although of course they knew my story there, and really it was none of their business what I now, as a free woman, did with the money that was rightfully mine, still I shrank from thus exposing myself to widespread speculation and comment.

Of course I could always say I wanted the money to buy a house in London. In fact that might be quite a good plan. For several days my fancy played happily around the idea of buying a really beautiful little town house—Hampstead or St. John's Wood perhaps—bringing Malcolm in to advise on decorating and equipping and perfecting it, and then, with a fairy godmother-like wave of the wand, setting it before Judy as her very own. I elaborated the daydream, on

my walk to work, while I sat eating a sandwich meal in the
Russell Square gardens, where the roses were beginning to
bloom and the shrubs were thick, puffed out with the bright
full foliage of early summer; as I sat by my window and let
my eyes rest with grateful recognition on the familiar shapes
and colours of the square. I even took a bus to St. John's
Wood and wandered dreamily about the leafy side streets,
their pretty, exclusive villas alternating with great blocks of
luxury flats. For brief moments I recaptured something of
the spirit of happiness that had come to me on my arrival in
London, after I had first seen Judy.

But it was a pale echo, a nostalgic aftermath. The
twilight, not the dawn. It was overladen, and soon it was
eclipsed, by the dread reality: that I must save my secret,
and in order to save my secret, Malcolm must go.

He would not go of his own accord and I had no
conceivable means of persuading him. He might have an
accident. His car was powerful and he was a reckless driver.
But I could not count on it. Unless it happened that
something was wrong with his car. That was a possibility,
but it would take a lot of thinking out. It was Friday evening
when this thought struck me, and Friday was his regular day
for visiting the Prescotts. I could hear all three of them next
door, chatting noisily. I got up and moved to the window, as
if to derive inspiration from it, pulled up the sash a few feet
with the help of Tom's contraption, and bent down to step
out on to the balcony.

My little plants in their great heavy pots were bushy and
healthy, showing tantalising glimpses of purple and blue
and pink. There would be a lovely show before long, I
thought with an irrelevant pleasure. But one of them was
rather too close to the rail—that broken rail at the corner.
"You will be very careful, won't you, Miss Wentworth,"
old Mrs. Willows in the basement had begged me when I
told her how I proposed to use the balcony. "You'll make
sure and be very careful. They're not safe, those balconies.

The railings are rusty too. You don't want to stand too near
the edge—nearly had a nasty accident once—nice young
chap too . . ."

Her refined and quavering voice had droned on and on,
telling me how time and again she had begged the owner of
the house to do something about the balconies, or forbid
people to use them altogether, but to no avail. I could recall
it well, that conversation, and one word of it now stood out
particularly clearly in my mind; an accident, a nasty
accident. That great flowerpot, earth-filled, that could kill a
man. I eased it slowly towards the corner where the broken
rail was. What a weight it was! I looked up and around the
square; there were a few people about, but no one was
looking in my direction. Why should they? I was a familiar
enough sight, bending lovingly over my plants. I was a
well-known form, a little splash of colour in the view from
somebody else's window. I pushed the pot a little nearer.
Would it go through the gap? Not quite, but the rails there
were so weak and brittle that it would need very little
pressure to make them bend or snap. And then the pot
would go through easily, tilt over easily with just one final
firm push. Should I leave it there and then await my
moment? Would not somebody notice how near the edge it
was and draw attention to its dangerous position?

I stood hesitant, clinging to the raised sash of the great
window behind me. And then I heard the cheerful voices,
this time sounding from the front doorsteps beneath the
balcony, and then I saw Tom and Judy run round to the
other side of the white sports car, and I leaned forward,
holding on ever more tightly to the sash, and just below my
balcony was the head of thick hair and the brown suèded
shoulders underneath, and my foot came up to the rim of the
flowerpot and it kicked, and with the effort and the strain
and the attempt not to fall myself, my hand came down too
hard on the edge of the sash window, and Tom's contraption

gave way, and the great weight came crashing down and I with it.

I lay sprawled across the balcony, crushing the plants, my feet protruding through the gap where the great flowerpot had gone, my arm, slipped from the window, gripping the rails at the other end in an effort to save myself. There were screams and there were shouts, and the triple crash, of the flowerpot, the window, and myself, seemed to resound into eternity. Some of the screams were my own, and they were for help. I was trapped, bruised and helpless, unable to shift myself, a prisoner on a rickety bit of old iron, locked out from safety by a vast and immovable window. I screamed and screamed.

"Help, help! It's going, it's giving way! I can't move! Can't move!"

It went on for ever, and then for a short while I think I was unconscious, and then it began once more, and my cries were so loud that they had to shout again and again from inside the window in order to be heard:

"It's all right—we're coming! Hold on! You'll be all right if you hold on."

They came and went, sometimes louder, sometimes almost inaudible, and my fingers gripping the rail seemed to be torn through and through with the iron. My arms ached, my whole body was encased in pain, I longed to sleep.

"Can you hear me? Can you hear me, Miss Wentworth?"

I recognised the voice, the faint northern accent. What was Dr. Strangeways doing there shouting at my bedside? I made some movement. His voice went on:

"We can't shift the window—the fire brigade are coming—here they come now. They'll get you off from below. Hold on, hold on!"

Suddenly the world was full of men in dark uniforms. I watched it as if it were a cinema screen. It was an unusual and exciting rescue and it did not take very long.

"Are you all right, ma'am? Can you stand? Are you in pain?"

The open back of the ambulance gaped in front of me. I struggled upright out of the fireman's grasp. My foot knocked against some hard fragments on the pavement—what were these stones doing there, I wondered, and then I stood firm, took one step, then another, moved one arm, then the other.

I looked around the circle of faces and I smiled. "No bones broken—only dreadfully sore."

"You'd better come along to Casualty, ma'am, all the same." It was the voice of authority.

"Why, yes," I smiled again, "I do feel bruised—black and blue all over. Can I just go upstairs a minute, please—just to the bathroom, and to fetch my bag?"

"I'll come with you, then."

I was glad of his help. He was a nice, fresh-faced, sturdy youngster. I crept painfully up the stairs, and in the bathroom I let cold water run over my lacerated hands. The pain intensified, and it cleared my mind. My handbag, that was the only thing. It contained my driving licence, with my real name on it. Nothing else in the room mattered. My working papers were innocent; only a few sheets of instruction from Professor Barlow lay among them—no names, no personal comments, no clues. No photographs. No books. Since the Cornwall anthology was discovered, I had been through everything, and made doubly sure. They could search my room, they could do their will. But my driving licence, passport to my greatest pleasure—that I must regain. How strange it was, I thought, as the nice fireman helped me up the rest of the stairs after I had been in the bathroom, that after Robert's death, after my trial and acquittal, no one had thought to deprive me of the means by which his death had come about; my licence had never even been endorsed; it was clean, virginal, and also tell-tale. It bore my name; it was valid for another six months at least.

I barely looked at my room. The handbag was on the table, untouched, as I had left it. I picked it up, looked inside and muttered something about finding a comb because I must look such a sight.

"Ah, you ladies," said the fireman indulgently. "Always the first thing you think of is your lipsticks."

I laughed dutifully. I had checked that the licence—*my* licence—was there, and I was content.

"Oh well," I said, and then the faintness overcame me and I would have fallen had it not been for his steadying hand.

"Come on, ma'am. Is there anything else you'd like to take?"

"No, thank you," I struggled to say. "If they keep me in—but I'm sure they won't—my neighbour will bring me anything I need, I expect."

My neighbour. My neighbour Judy. Where was she? Where were they all? Where was—I hardly dared frame the name even in my mind—where was Malcolm?

Faintness gave way to hysteria.

"What happened?" I cried to the fireman. "How long had I been there? What happened?"

"Now take it easy, ma'am. What happened is just what we'd all like to know. But first of all you want to get those hands looked at and those bruises seen to."

"But I must talk to someone! I *must*!"

"You'll see the doctor—won't be long now, ma'am."

"Is he—is he . . . "

Is he dead, I wanted to ask, meaning Malcolm. It was fortunate that the effort of moving had temporarily taken my breath away.

"The doctor, ma'am?" said the fireman as he handed me over to the ambulance attendant. "Yes, he'll be there, at the hospital. You'll be seeing him very soon now."

All right. So I was an idiot child. So I knew nothing. If they wanted it that way, all right. But I did notice this much before I was taken away, that the white sports car stood just in front of the door, as it had earlier, and the ambulance and the fire engine had had to park a few yards farther down the road.

10

How restful it is to be sucked into the great womb of impersonal kindness that is the modern hospital at its best! The nurse who took my particulars wasted no time. Name? Age? Address? I answered wearily.

The doctor was a young Indian, not unlike one of the students who lived on the top floor. Or did I think this because all Indians look alike to Western eyes? I did not make any protest when he told me they would find me a bed for the night, so that I could get over the shock. It was at the far end of a long ward, and they drew the curtains round it. Light curtains, rather dingy. I lay in a voluminous hospital nightgown. It was clean, but rather dingy too. The clothes I had been wearing were folded up in the locker by the side of my bed; my handbag stood on top of it.

And that was all there was of myself, all there was left of this thing we call personality, the myriad impressions of people and circumstances, the odds and ends of information, the carefully acquired skills, the worldly possessions, the memories, the hopes and the fears. It was as if I was back in the prison cell. It was small and comforting. It was safe.

And there I lay, interested now in the shocking colours on my arm and shoulder, the throbbing in my thigh, the sting

113

of my bandaged hands. I dozed, and woke to a cup of Ovaltine and a different face over the starched apron. And then I slept for a very long time and had no dreams, and when I woke it was as if I had been on a journey of many years and lost all touch with the people I had left behind me. I blinked, unrecognising, at the pale face that leant over me, wondering why there was no uniform, why the fair hair was allowed to stray in such an untidy manner.

"Miss Wentworth! Miss Wentworth!"

I blinked again. The nurses called me "Luv" or "Dear." All part of this great, impersonal security.

"Miss Wentworth! Don't you know me? They didn't say you had concussion. You are all right, aren't you?"

I struggled to sit up. My eyes were wide open now. "Oh Judy, oh Judy!"

And I burst into tears.

"Here you are," she exclaimed triumphantly, and whisked out a box of Kleenex from a large carrier bag. "I knew you'd want some—wasn't I right?"

She was, for once. I took the tissues gratefully.

"And I've brought you a nice nightie—I hope you didn't mind me opening your chest of drawers, but I thought you'd like to have it—and your brush and comb and spongebag. And a little towel—I think hospital ones are normally rather drear."

"Oh Judy!" I could only cry out weakly and dab at my eyes.

"And a clean pair of stockings—I expect yours are torn to shreds—though I daresay you won't need them for a day or two—and I didn't bring any flowers, I'm afraid, as I didn't pass any shops or barrows on the way."

"My dear child! You needn't have done so much. But I'm tremendously grateful—I can't tell you how much." My sobbing voice failed for a moment. "I expect I'll be back home today," I went on, after a moment or two.

"Oh, I don't expect they'll let you out for a few days,"

she said lightly. "You've had a frightful shock, you know. It must have been awful—stuck up there on that balcony like that. Absolutely ghastly. I'd have been terrified out of my wits."

She spoke with a certain relish, and I made no response. Then Malcolm must be alive, I was telling myself. If Malcolm were dead, she could not come here chatting to me brightly like this. She would be too upset; it would affect her too deeply. If Malcolm were dead, she would have blamed me, not in the sense that she would have suspected me of killing him, but she would have held me responsible for the accident of his death. I owed her present kindness to my own failure. I did not know whether to be glad or sorry that Malcolm was still alive. Here, in this dingy but light sanctuary, it seemed of little importance. Perhaps I was glad, really, although I wished him gone. It was so difficult to remember, so long ago. Had I really tried to kill him? I had thought of it, thought of him having an accident in his car. And after that, all was confused.

"Tom feels rather awful about it," Judy was saying, "because in a way it was his fault really, that his pulley thing wasn't strong enough. He shouldn't have let you use it. He ought to have got a proper builder in or something."

"Pulley thing?" I echoed in bewilderment.

"Yes—that's why the sash came down when you grabbed it when you slipped. It gave way, and of course you had nothing to break your fall. It's a wonder it wasn't worse—that you didn't go right over the edge, or the balcony come away altogether."

The pleased little note of horror was still in her voice. I leant back and covered my face with my hands. "Judy," I said, "I'm so muddled. It's all like a nightmare. I can't remember what happened."

It sounded natural, I hoped, but behind my muttered words my mind was singing with relief; thank you, thank you, Judy, for telling me the way. Of course that's how it was; of course it is. I slipped and I grabbed to save myself, and kicked the pot over the edge as I fell. When I tell my story—as tell it I must—that is what I shall say. Thank you, Judy, beautiful guardian angel; thank you.

"I remember trying to get hold of the window," I said after a suitable pause, "and falling, and a terrible crash—oh a terrible crash—and then, well it's a bit confused after that. Didn't part of the balcony break away?"

"No. Well—not really. Only a railing or two. And the flowerpot came down, of course."

I sat up and cried out in horror: "The flowerpot! Good God! They're a frightful weight. It didn't hurt anyone, did it?"

She looked a trifle embarrassed, I thought, but at the same time gave a smug little smile.

"Well, as a matter of fact it did. I wasn't going to tell you, actually. They said you weren't to be upset."

Hurry up, girl, hurry up, I said to myself while I held my pose. Is he injured? Let me know at once—is he badly injured?

"I'm not upset," I said aloud. "For heaven's sake tell me what happened—I can't stand this not knowing."

"Well—Malcolm was standing bang underneath—and he must have heard you slip or the window start to move or something because luckily he happened to look up and move slightly, and the pot just touched his head slightly and caught his shoulder. Otherwise it could have killed him—if it had gone full on his head."

She looked at me with lovely eyes wide with horror, and this time there was no relish in it. I felt a crazy, furious stab of jealousy. My own sufferings evoked pleasurable excitement as well as sympathy, but Malcolm's death was sheer tragedy. It was unfair. I slipped down against the pillows and my eyes began to fill again.

"There, you see, it *did* upset you," said Judy. "I knew you ought not to be told."

Her complacency was insufferable.

"Was he badly hurt?" I asked, controlling myself with an effort.

"I don't think there's anything actually broken," was the reply, "but he has slight concussion and it's injured his shoulder quite badly. I'm not quite sure what they call it, but he's got to keep his arm in a sling quite a while. It's his right arm, unfortunately, so it'll be difficult for him to work, but we shall help him all we can, of course. I'll do his typing, and Tom can drive him—he won't be able to drive for ages."

"I'm terribly sorry," I said, and somehow I managed to put some warmth into my voice, although the idea of Judy caring so tenderly for Malcolm brought with it a grinding ache, "I feel—I feel somehow to blame."

"Oh please, Miss Wentworth, don't *you* start! Tom's bad enough, worrying about that wretched window. It wasn't your fault in the least. You couldn't possibly have helped the window breaking and you slipping and knocking the pot off! It could have happened to anyone. It was an awful accident, but it might have been ever so much worse."

It might, I thought; we might both have been dead. Or would that have been worse? Would not that be the best way out? There could be nothing in life for me now; I would have no regrets at leaving it. But to leave Judy to Malcolm—no, that I could not do. So Tom was driving Malcolm's car, was he? The germ of a scheme began to form in my head, but I would not allow it to develop yet. I wanted my little time of peace.

"Where is Malcolm?" I asked, seeking to divert my own thoughts. "He wasn't in the ambulance with me—or in the Casualty here. At least, I don't think so, but I wasn't very much in a state to notice."

"Oh no," she said. "They took ages getting you off—but Tom brought Malcolm straight round to the hospital in a taxi—he's in the other wing from you—the surgical wing.

They did lots of X-rays and things last night—took ages and ages over them—before we were allowed to see him."

Icy drops, horrible stabs of steel, worse than all the aches in my body was this torment of jealousy. She had been here, here in this very building where I lay. She had gone first to Malcolm and not to me. It was intolerable; it was beyond endurance.

"They wouldn't let us come near you either," she went on. "They said I wasn't to come along till this morning as you were too shocked to see visitors."

The cold sickness eased away, leaving me weaker than ever, in wretched resentment that I should be caught up so helplessly in this endless switchback of jealousy and relief. I must bring it to an end, finish it for ever; next time I must not fail. And I must not leave it too long.

When Judy had gone I tried to force my weary mind to look ahead and plan. I must not leave it too long. I could not stand it, and, even more important, delay was dangerous. I had got away with one accident, but I dared not risk another failure. The young policeman who appeared at my bedside to take a statement drove home this point to me. He was a nice, friendly lad; not unlike the fireman who had taken me off the balcony.

The nurses did not allow him to remain for long. My shock and my distress were not assumed, and I could barely speak. I told him feebly that I could only remember trying to drag the flowerpot away from the edge of the balcony, to which it looked to me to be dangerously near, and it was a very great weight and I must have slipped and overbalanced and I clutched at the window and it came down with a crash, and that was all I knew. And, yes, Mr. Prescott had very kindly arranged this pulley affair to get the window up and down, and yes again I was indeed desperately sorry that I had put flowerpots on the balcony at all, but I had asked the caretaker, and I had been told that there was no objection, provided I was very careful, and I had had so much pleasure from my flowers, and it was just *because* I was trying to be so careful that . . .

At this point I wept unrestrainedly. He waited stolidly, and then asked me to read through and sign the statement that he had been laboriously writing out in longhand. I did so, shakily. Mary Wentworth. It was accepted without question. And why not indeed? It is assumed that one gives the real name unless it is proved to the contrary. There was no question of anything criminal here; no question of prosecution. I was the victim of an accident for which nobody could be held to blame. It was, if anyone, the owner of the property who was at fault, for allowing the balconies to remain in such a dangerous condition, for not warning his tenants right off their use. In fact—and as my fear receded I was borne up by indignation—in fact I probably had a case for suing them for damages. It might be a good idea, on getting home, to go straight into the attack. The idea revived me, and neutralised the shock of the policeman's visit. I composed a letter of complaint in my mind, as was my wont, neatly and incisively shifting the burden of responsibility on to the owner of the house. But I was half-hearted about it; it did not really interest me. I knew the letter would never be sent; there were far more important matters to attend to.

I remained so weak and feverish that they kept me several days in the hospital. I was glad of this. It gave me a chance to rest my tired body, gather my mental strength, build up my plans, the plans that would end it all. Judy came each evening, and her visits were a mixture of torment and of great joy. If she had been to see Malcolm before coming to me, then I was wild because she preferred to go to him first. If she came to me before seeing Malcolm then I was in despair, because obviously visiting me was a tedious chore that she wanted to get out of the way before she had the pleasure of visiting him.

Her movements grated on me, and she was always flustered and hot and slightly sweating, because she rushed

straight from her office to the hospital. She was officious
and self-righteous and she had nothing to say that contained
the least scrap of wit or cleverness or originality or humour.
She was never so welcome as at that first moment when
surprisingly she had had the imagination and the sense to
bring me a packet of Kleenex. And yet the gangrenous,
disease-ridden soldiers of the Crimea could not have felt a
greater uplift of adoration and senseless joy when the Lady
with the Lamp came within their vision, as I did when I saw
Judy approach my bed. "Thou art my life, my love, my
heart, the very eyes of me—and hast command of every part
to live and die for thee." And so you have, Judy, you silly
little ignorant slut, who have probably never heard of
Robert Herrick, unless you were once forced to learn "To
Daffodils" as a punishment at school.

Alice would know, though. But Alice is a plain and rigid
girl with an unattractive mouth.

Alice came to see me, too, the last evening, just as Judy
was going, and the looks they gave each other amused and
gladdened me. But it was a bore to have to talk to Alice.
Her pity was infuriating, and our learned conversations at
the Museum seemed to belong to another world. She did,
however, enlighten me on one point that I had been
strangely reluctant to put to Judy. To my great surprise, my
second day in hospital I received a card from my elderly
friends in Hampstead Garden Suburb. The envelope was
sealed, and on it was written simply my name and that of
the hospital. The "W" of Wentworth looked to me suspi-
ciously as if it had begun as an "H," but the writing was old
and shaky, and I did not think it could be visible to any other
eye. Inside was a conventional, floral "Get well" card, and
on the back Aunt Laura had written:

"Very sorry to hear about your accident, Mary, and hope
you are well looked after and will soon be all right again.
You must be careful and never put yourself into such a
dangerous situation again—it might have been a very nasty
accident indeed."

The last sentence was underlined three times. I did not know what to make of it, and above all I could not understand how they had come to hear about it at all. I showed the card to Alice, taking care not to let her see the message on the back.

"However did they find out? I never wrote—and they don't know any of my friends and neighbours in Bloomsbury."

"Why, from the paper, of course," said Alice with a faint air of contempt. Obviously the design on the card would not have been her own choice. "There was quite a little story about it. It wasn't in all the papers, of course."

"Oh." I lay thinking about this with great anxiety. "I never saw it."

"I expect the nurses were told not to let you see—you probably weren't in a fit state," said Alice primly.

"But the others in the ward—it's funny nobody mentioned it or came near me."

"I expect they were warned not to—and anyway, knowing you, Miss Wentworth, I'm sure you had your curtains drawn round you most of the time!"

It was said with an attempt at a smile, obviously intended as an intimate little joke about my love of privacy, which I had been foolish enough on one occasion to confess to her. But it didn't come off; it sounded forced and impudent; it showed the girl at her worst, and I wished I would never have to see her again. She flushed slightly at the enquiring, eyebrow-raised look I gave her, and then said:

"There were pictures, too—pretty poor ones. But it must have been very terrifying."

"Pictures! How horrible and undignified! I was carried down a ladder by firemen, I believe. Oh Alice, this really *does* distress me—to think that millions of people may have seen such—such beastly photographs of me! I only hope my face wasn't visible—or that at any rate it was as blurred as most press photos are."

Very anxiously I awaited her reply.

"Oh no—I don't think any of them showed your face at all. It was just a sort of jumbled-up black splodge."

"Thank God!" I said with a fervour that she would only half comprehend, and I was so relieved that I was even able to feel mildly surprised that she had dropped her normal manner of speech and fallen into a slangy sloppiness that was not unworthy of Judy. She talked a little more, but I responded absentmindedly. An idea had occurred to me.

"I was wondering, Alice, if you could do me a great favour. I don't feel very inclined to get back to work just yet, but I've promised Professor Barlow to let him have the rest of the letters by the end of next week. Would you care to—would you be allowed to work on late for some evenings or in your lunch break and do the copying for me? Of course I'd pay you my fee. I'm sure you'll know which bits to extract—we've talked about it so much. I'd be extremely grateful if you could. It really is worrying me a lot."

She jumped at it. She liked—or needed—money very much; I knew that. We discussed the necessary arrangements and I suggested that, to save time, she should forward the transcripts direct to him. I would write and explain meanwhile.

After she had gone I lay back, relieved. It was all sorting itself out nicely now. There remained only to perfect my final plan. Of course I did not really intend killing myself too, or rather, I would only do so if there were no other way. But I had to act on the assumption that it could end that way and, while I was not interested in making any testamentary dispositions, and did not care in the least what cousins, many times removed, would benefit from Robert's considerable fortune, I did care very much that Professor Barlow should not suffer in any way from any omission of mine. But that was now attended to, and there would be no need for me ever to see Alice, or even to visit the Museum, again.

11

It was strange, when the taxi drew up at the house in the square, to reflect that I was coming home. I did not think, judging from Judy's visits and her conversation, that anyone had the least suspicion of me or the least doubt that the accident was just what it seemed to be, but all the same I was nervous about meeting my fellow lodgers, and was glad to reach the sanctuary of my own room.

At first sight it appeared exactly as I had left it, and then I noticed a few unmistakable signs that Judy had been there. The cushions were slightly dented and badly placed, the divan cover hung unevenly, a drawer was not quite closed, and a bunch of anemones had been thrust into a vase much too big for them. It irritated me. I had to put everything back as it ought to be, although I was very exhausted and wanted only to rest. One new touch, however, was not Judy's work. A large square of cardboard, stuck to the window with cellotape, had written on it in large red capitals: DO NOT TRY TO OPEN. I pulled it off more annoyed than ever. Who had stuck it there? Whom was it meant for? As if *I* would try to open the window! And who else but I had a right to be in the room? I looked through the glass at the balcony. Except for the now gaping hole in the railings at one corner, it looked just as it had before, but very empty.

For a moment I was puzzled. The rest of my view was the same, just as I had left it. And then it dawned on me. The other flowerpots were gone. My carefully tended petunias and lobelia and Virginia stocks, just beginning to show promise of their brightness and gaiety, they had all been taken away.

I was furious, shaking with anger. Who was interfering in my life like this, removing my possessions without permission? It was intolerable. I was about to run downstairs and challenge the old caretaker, demand an explanation. And then I remembered that my position in the house might not be very agreeable now; there would be awkwardness, and they might even want me to leave. But it's their fault for not keeping the property in decent repair, I stormed to myself. Do you want them to look too closely into the accident, my reason countered. It was no good. I must accept any insult, put up with any interference, just so long as I could stay here—as stay here I must—till my plan was ready and the moment had come and it would all be at an end.

Judy came in that evening, with a few bits and pieces of shopping for me, and I was yet once again dissolved in maudlin tears of gratitude, and of guilt for my unkind thoughts about her. I asked after Malcolm.

"He's home too," she said, "and his charwoman's doing a lot for him but I promised to go up this evening and get him a meal."

I swallowed my jealousy and praised her kindness. She had spoken simply and sincerely, with no self-righteous complacency in her voice. She looked tired and pale, and no wonder. Why, I thought with amazement, I believe you are just an ordinary little kind-hearted girl who puts herself out for people she likes, even if it means doing other people's shopping as well as your own, and running about after your day's work getting other people's meals, as well as looking after your husband's. Yes, you're a good little thing, I thought, and there's room in the world for simple, unimag-

inative, unselfish people such as you. And I looked at her
skimpy summer frock in the pink she loved so well and that
suited her so badly, and it did not bother me in the least; and
then I looked at her hands as she was taking my shopping
out of the bag, and I noticed with pity and without disgust
that the nails were dirty and the polish cracked and peeling,
and something very strange stirred deep within me, something of the feeling I had had when I realised that my old
Uncle Jimmy was confused in his mind and believed Robert
to be still alive, some sort of grief at the pathos and the
helplessness and the unawareness of humanity, and I
wanted to warn her, put her on her guard.

It lasted only a moment or two. She placed the eggs she
had brought in the bowl where I usually kept them, and,
clumsy as ever, cracked one of them as she did so. Then she
gave me a sideways glance, half frightened, half hoping I
had not noticed, and all my old feelings came flooding
back—the irritation, the yearning, the triumph in my power
to hurt, the sickening cringing knowledge that she had the
power to hurt me, and when she left me to go to Malcolm,
the lump of fury arose in my throat and I promised myself
release. It can't go on; you will end it soon, very soon.

But meanwhile there was much unpleasantness to face.
Old Mrs. Willows, I discovered, had been so upset by the
accident that she had been taken away in a state of collapse
by her daughter-in-law. A surly young man with a slatternly
pregnant wife had been put in her place. He made some
insinuating remarks which I briskly countered with com-
plaints about the condition of the property. How education
does tell! I soon shut him up.

"As if I would ever dream of trying to go on the balcony
again," I concluded, "or even of opening the window! After
an experience like that!"

There was an odd atmosphere in the house, all the same.
Dr. Strangeways greeted me in kindly enough manner:

"You certainly gave us all a fright—but yourself most of

all, I should think. Whatever induced you to try and shift those flowerpots yourself without help?"

"I thought they were a bit too near the edge," I said feebly.

He looked at me keenly, but said nothing and simply shook his head slightly.

"I—I'm awfully sorry to have caused such a commotion," I said.

"Ah well. It might have been a great deal worse. At least no one was killed."

"No, thank God."

I had very similar conversations with Dennis and Harry, and with Liz. I did not so much feel that they distrusted or disbelieved me as that, because of the accident, I had suddenly been translated into a realm outside their experience, had been turned by the event into another sort of being, with whom it was not possible to be on the same terms as before.

Judy alone treated me naturally, and indeed with great kindness. I flattered myself that this was because of her affection for me, but later on I realised that she was trying to make up for Tom's behaviour. I saw nothing of him for a day or two after I got home, and Judy told me he would be writing his exams the following week, and was very busy. I believed this excuse for his non-appearance until I saw him deliberately step back into his room when I opened my door, and wait until I was downstairs before emerging himself. It grieved me a little, but on reflection I was not surprised. After all, he ought not to have left the window in so unsafe a condition, and no doubt he had been held responsible for its giving way and had had a lot of tiresome explaining to do. My main interest in him was that his examinations might perhaps result in an opportunity for me to carry out my plan. It was always the initial problem of getting Malcolm to let me drive his car that had been the great stumbling block in all my scheming. But if Tom were shortly to be unavailable, that might not be so difficult.

He was going to fetch Malcolm in the car tomorrow, so Judy told me on the Friday evening after my return, just one week after the accident had occurred. And then Tom would bring him down for the whole Sunday, so that Judy could get his meals. But of course the following week would not be so easy, with Tom engaged so much, and she did so wish she herself could drive.

I nearly said it then, but bit it back just in time. It must come spontaneously, at the very right moment. Say a word to Judy now, and it would go straight to Tom, and then my chance would be lost for ever. Tom would prevent it somehow; there was no doubting his ill-will towards me. His own vanity as a handyman had been bitterly hurt and, even if he suspected me of no evil intent, still he could not forgive me for showing up his own inadequacies. Judy's present kindness towards me was probably an additional cause of annoyance. But he was not important. It was Malcolm who mattered, Malcolm who held my secret, whose suspicions must surely now be thoroughly aroused, who rivalled me in Judy's attention and who always, in the last resort, won more of it than I did myself; Malcolm whom I had injured, Malcolm who this time must die.

But how on earth to tempt him into letting me give him a lift in his car? What a problem this was! Somehow or other I would have to make it plain, without words, that I was offering myself up to his mercy. I must appeal to his cruelty and his vanity and his sense of power, by hinting very strongly that I was going to confess, give myself up, let him do as he wished with me. That ought to do the trick. I would somehow be able to get it across, even with others present. He was far from stupid; he would understand.

I was amazed, in the end, how easy it was, even without any such hints. The foundations were laid on that very Friday, a week after the window collapsed. I listened to them all next door, chattering away as usual, and then when Tom went on ahead to start up the car, I opened my door at the very moment that Judy and Malcolm came out to follow, and I gave a good start of surprise.

"Ah—Miss Wentworth. The other victim. Quite a little drama, wasn't it? A nice little bonus for the tabloids on a day without much news."

He was as bland and mocking as ever. The broad white sling was tied over a beautiful navy Italian sweater; the thick brown hair was brushed over at an unusual angle and, I guessed, hid the external evidence of the head injury. Only the blue eyes looked slightly less clear, and this was because they were ringed with darker blue. He smiled at me, and the lines were more deeply etched. Nigel Reeves doing a gallant suffering stunt, I thought suddenly, but when he moved along the landing I could see that he was indeed in pain and far from well. And Judy cares, I thought furiously, she cares more than she cares about me.

"I don't know what to say," I said, "I feel so dreadful about it—I feel so responsible—I ought never to have gone on the balcony at all . . ."

He held up his good hand: "Please, please, Miss Wentworth. We're having quite enough of this sort of thing from Tom. Don't you start too. Let's be grateful it was no worse. After all, *my* part of the business was very rapidly over. *Your* sufferings were more long drawn out."

Pleasantly said, but I sensed the hidden threat. Never mind: by taking it this way he was going to make it easier for me. Of course he had a new hold now, a fresh source of knowledge with which to threaten and torment me; he was evidently going to take it easy until he was recovered himself, until he felt fit to launch a new and much more terrible campaign. But the time would never come. I had him now.

"It was probably worse for me at the time," I said, "but its effects have not been so long-lasting."

He glanced down at his arm, and I thought I saw him wince and look unhappy like a small boy.

"Too true. It is inconvenient, I admit. But I gather recovery is counted in weeks rather than months, which is always a blessing."

I made a conventional reply, and I saw Judy look first at him and then at me, and her look said as plainly as if she had spoken that she greatly admired Malcolm for making so light of it in order to spare my feelings, and I knew then that they had discussed me often, the two of them, analysing me, deciding on this line of deliberate kindness towards me, congratulating themselves on standing out from the others as more sympathetic and understanding; enjoying, perhaps, being in league together against Tom. And where was all my nice little fantasy of taking Judy to pieces with Malcolm's help? Were not the tables turned? Was it not I who was the object of pity? Once more the blind fury seized me, mingled with jealousy and with fear. For Malcolm was double-crossing Judy too. He was playing this little game with her until the moment came for his ultimate aim—his ultimate triumph: the exposure of myself.

I did not know how to endure the days until it could end. I had my plan, but it depended so much on circumstance, on what other people did. The waiting was more terrible than anything I had ever experienced before. But it had to be; it was now the only way.

On the Wednesday the chance came. I gathered from Judy, who always looked in on me on her return from work to see if I was all right, that Tom was very depressed and irritable about his exams, and that he was going straight on this evening to have a few drinks with a fellow sufferer and indulge in a mournful post mortem. She was rather annoyed, because Malcolm was coming down by taxi, and Tom had promised to drive him home, and now he would probably be very late and she didn't think Malcolm ought to have to wait so long. The car was, as I had already noticed, parked more or less permanently the other side of the square. Still I held my tongue. It could still go wrong; I must wait until I was quite, quite sure.

"So I'll have to get him a taxi," said Judy after giving me a chance to speak, and she went on to suggest that I join them for a meal. I excused myself. I was very nervous and tired still, not much fit for company. I thought she gave me a contemptuous look as she left the room; if Malcolm can make an effort and put a bright face on it, why can't you, she seemed to say. But I did not care. Above all I must not be too eager. To be reluctant at first was part of the plan.

It went like clockwork. I stationed myself by the head of my bed, in the corner where the two ramshackle partitions were so inadequately joined, and where I could actually hear some of the words spoken next door, though not, unfortunately, enough to catch the gist of the conversation. But I heard them sit down to eat, and turn on the radio—a pop song far too loud—and I guessed Malcolm's comment, and that Judy had switched over to an orchestral concert, and then little was said, and then they cleared away the plates and I think Judy protested that he shouldn't be trying to carry things. And then the talking stopped while the sound of running water told me that Judy was washing up. And then there was some more music, and some more talk.

Nine-thirty. Why did he not go? It was getting late; Tom might yet come back in time. The minutes passed and I could scarcely breathe. The thought of failure, of having to go through all this again, was choking me. I must act now. Now or never.

I combed my hair and washed my hands. I went to the Prescotts' door and knocked. As on the very first occasion when I did so, Judy opened the door. She looked as beautiful as she had done then, and as untidy as ever. Her eyes were melting, her smile was sweetness itself. And yet she was different. She looked thinner, older, perhaps even

more mature. Estelle, my mind cried out, Estelle. This is
how you came to look—this is just the same.

"I'm sorry to interrupt," I said, "but I was wondering, if
Tom hasn't come back yet, whether Malcolm would like me
to run him home. I've not driven for some time, but I've
always been very careful. If he'll trust me I dare say I can
manage to Hampstead. I'll come back by tube, of course."

It was perfect. Judy was all over me. Malcolm was
grateful. Taxis were a nuisance—you could never be sure of
finding one, and to try and phone for one was hopeless.
He'd show me the controls—the car was simple enough to
drive. He seemed to have no thought in his mind other than
getting home in comfort. A brilliant actor, I thought, and
then, irrelevantly: my parents would have admired him,
they would have appreciated his gifts. But his skills had
deprived me of the exercise of mine, and I felt almost
cheated that I had no need to put into effect my scheme for
hinting to him that he had won, that I yielded up the game
to him. Still, he was coming, and that was the main thing.

And then Judy nearly went and spoiled everything.

"It's a nice evening," she said in her most ordinary way,
"and if Miss Wentworth's driving I'm sure we'll be very
safe and slow. I think I'll come along too."

My whole being cried out—No, no! But I could not think
of a single reason why she should not join us. I had stupidly
not anticipated this, and my invention failed me. Malcolm
came to the rescue. It was too funny; it might have been
tailor-made for me.

"Well, duckie, that's very noble of you, but don't you
think it might be a little more tactful to be here when Tom
gets back?"

As if *he's* ever cared about being tactful towards Tom, I
thought, remembering the birthday party, and it occurred to
me that he did after all understand my purpose, that I
wanted to be with him alone.

"Oh all right," said Judy as she saw us to the car. "I

expect you're right. Have a good drive." She beamed on me
with approval, but she blew a kiss at Malcolm.

The car was easy enough to handle. After a slight initial
awkwardness with the gear change, I was perfectly confi-
dent.

"Well, you have got the hang of it very quickly," said
Malcolm. "Much better than Tom. I always said you were
a good driver."

"It's a gorgeous car."

We talked about it for a few moments as if we were two
old friends. Hampstead first, I thought; let him suspect
nothing yet.

"I hope you didn't think I was a bit abrupt just now with
our friend Judy," he said, "especially in view of the
unfortunate results when you acted rather similarly yourself
on a recent occasion. But to tell the truth, I've had about as
much of her as I can take just lately. One is very trapped
with this business"—and he indicated his injured arm—
"and I'm extremely grateful to her. She has given me a lot
of time and trouble and there aren't many people who would
do it. But there are times—well, I don't need to explain to
you, Miss Wentworth. I'm sure—without being ungrateful
or disloyal—that you know exactly what I mean."

"Yes, indeed." I spoke with sympathy. I could have
laughed aloud. Here we were, on the very edge of bringing
my little fantasy into being; a cosy analysis of Judy's
character alongside a clever and observant man. But I must
not be distracted from my purpose. All this was to throw
dust in my eyes, no doubt, to disarm suspicion. He was
threatening, dangerous; he must be got rid of.

"I'm very fond of them both," he went on, "but they do
irritate me sometimes into doing things that I'm ashamed of
afterwards. They do so expect me to strike a pose and be a
terrific personality that sometimes I fall into the trap and do
it—and it only offends people and leads to trouble. I wish I
could stop, but there's something about them—about Judy

in particular—that makes me behave like that. Sort of schoolboy show-off. I do wish I could understand why and then I might be able to stop it."

I hardly heard him. We were nearing Chalk Farm now. Along the A1, I thought, along the A1.

"I wouldn't talk to you like this," continued Malcolm, "if it weren't that I believe you feel rather as I do. I mean this business of Judy affecting you in such a way that you show off and then regret it. I was wondering if you had any idea why. It interests me a lot, and I'd like to hear what you think."

I heard the words, but they scarcely registered. Who does he think he's kidding, I asked myself impatiently. How long is he going to keep up this stupid pretence?

"So that's the line, is it?" I was becoming annoyed. "You've given up the Parry Barlow angle."

"Parry Barlow?" he repeated in astonishment. "What's he got to do with it?"

"Weren't you trying to get me to admit to you how well I knew Parry Barlow?"

"Oh God, yes, I was, wasn't I? I'm not surprised you're rather annoyed about it, and I'd like to apologise. You see, I'd been wondering for some time whether I couldn't get an exclusive interview—it would be a hell of a scoop. And somehow or other I had the impression—I don't quite know why—that you knew him rather better than you were going to let on. But I quite understand that if you do know him, you feel you have got to protect him—he being what he is—and I must keep my revolting journalist's headhunting to myself. I'm sorry. Honestly I am."

A likely story! Oh, he was clever, clever!

"Hold it—just a minute—where are we going?" he added in a different tone of voice. We had passed his turning and were speeding down towards Swiss Cottage. I controlled my voice and injected a little ingratiation.

"I just wondered if you'd mind—it's such a heavenly car

and I'm enjoying it so much. Could we run a mile or two up along Hendon Way and back?"

"Oh all right. If you like. But don't be too late. I really do want to get home."

I waited until we were clear of the worst traffic in Finchley Road. Had it not been for his injured arm, I might have felt nervous myself, for the cornered blackmailer can be a dangerous beast, and I didn't want a messy collision, with both of us injured but still alive. For I too must die. I knew that now. And what I could not do to myself in cold blood, I might perhaps achieve in the height of exhilaration of driving this wonderful car. I had to choose my moment, though; to make sure. Meanwhile there was a little time to kill, a little interval in which I could satisfy my own curiosity about how much he actually did know, and also to give myself the relief—the most blessed and wonderful relief—of talking freely to someone about it at last.

I made a few trivial remarks about the car.

"If you'd like to drop me back home now," he said, "you're most welcome to borrow it for an hour or two, as you're enjoying it so much. You are obviously a first-class driver, and I'd trust you with it completely. But really, Miss Wentworth, I am rather tired and I should be obliged if you would kindly turn at the next opportunity and drive me home."

I murmured something inaudible. The Brent flyover. With luck now we should be on the clearway within a few minutes, and then there would be no reason for stopping, no possibility, in fact. And then I was safe for hours. Plenty of time for talk and not the least risk, at the speed this car could go, of his trying to stop me even if he had not a useless right arm.

"I want to talk to you," I said as soon as I had settled down comfortably to the driving, so that it required very little attention and I could concentrate on the matter in hand. "When did you first guess who I really was?"

"Guess who you really were?" he repeated blankly, and I was annoyed at his obtuseness. What was going to be my relief, my satisfaction, in cornering him and telling my story, if he were going to play the innocent ignoramus in this stupid way?

"Oh, come off it!" I said in a vulgar manner. I was no longer afraid; there was no danger now of one of my earlier panic fears, because I knew what I had to do and I was borne up by the knowledge that I was the stronger now. But I was nervous, a little on edge, and it sounded in my voice. "What's the point of pretending now? You have nothing to gain. When did you guess that I was Mary Harmond?"

"Harmond, Harmond?" He repeated the name in the same silly way. "Harmond? On my God, yes! The War-mouth case. Of course. I remember now. I was abroad at the time, else I'd have been covering it, probably. I do cover murder trials from time to time for my sins."

I set my teeth. This was too much. It was more than absurd; it was intolerable, the way he was going on. I would have to give him a dose of his own medicine.

"Really?" I echoed. "Abroad, were you? Where?"

"West Germany—part business, part holiday. I wasn't troubling much about reading the papers there. But I do recall now that the verdict was given after my return. And we were all very glad about it—it would have been a dreadful miscarriage of justice—totally inadequate evidence, and obvious malice on the part of the chief prosecution witness—Derek, Dennis—whatever his name was."

"For one who had apparently forgotten all about the case," I said grimly, "you appear to be very well informed as to detail."

"Well—you know how it is—once one starts thinking about something it all begins to come back to mind. But, Miss Wentworth," he went on in an earnest voice, though I thought I scented something of anxiety in it behind his assumed surprise, "I would like to say that I very much admire your courage in trying to make a fresh start after such an appalling experience, and I can only assure you that as far as I am concerned your secret is perfectly safe. I am only sorry that you should have been worried by the supposition that I had guessed it—I can assure you that I had not the slightest idea, that I had never dreamed of connecting you with a case that I had in fact until this moment almost completely forgotten. You were simply a fellow lodger of Judy and Tom Prescott, a friend of theirs, a sophisticated and intelligent person—someone I was very glad to add to my acquaintance." He paused, obviously expecting a reply. I said nothing, but simply looked at the road ahead. Well out on the A1 now; not much traffic, a clear night, the road markings springing up brightly in the powerful headlamps. He spoke again:

"It is unfortunate that you should have felt it necessary to make this disclosure, since I am afraid you will find it difficult now to be at peace. I wish I could convince you that it is nothing to me—as far as I am concerned you are still Miss Wentworth as I first met you. I wouldn't dream of using your story professionally—damn it all, one isn't completely a swine! In fact, if there is anything at all I can do for you—if you want any introductions—socially or to do with your work . . . Oh, I do wish I could get it across to you that I really mean this and that your past is absolutely safe with me," he concluded in a voice half-irritable, half-despairing.

I began to feel a contempt for his intelligence. Was this what I had been so frightened of, what had driven me to panic, nearly out of my mind? This feeble, not very bright, would-be gentlemanlike middle-aged queer? Why, I even detected now, at last, a hint of something in his voice that betrayed his origins. Just a touch of the ugly Cockney whine that could come only from Australia.

"Where were you born?" I asked. "Sydney?"

After all, there was plenty of time. I was curious to see whether my guess was right.

"Yes," he said in surprise. "Whatever has that got to do with it?"

"I thought I could hear it in your speech. I'm rather good at accents."

"A veritable Professor Higgins."

How pompous, how stupidly affected, how *frightened* he sounded! He must have got an inkling by now; he must realise that he had played with me and tortured me too long. The worm had turned; the mouse now had the teeth. He did well to fear.

He was saying something about his childhood, about being early orphaned and coming to England and being thrilled to get a job on a provincial newspaper, and then about inheriting a lot of money from an uncle who had made a packet in manufacturing Christmas crackers and novelties, and he was rather ashamed of this, and did not like it to be generally known, although of course it was lovely to have the money, but he could quite understand what it felt like not to want people to know about your own past. I cut him short. My little spurt of curiosity was satisfied and I had no further interest in him. A silly, self-satisfied, pushing and snobbish colonial. He and Judy were on a par. Yes, they would suit each other very well. And what was I doing, racing northwards through the dark in this wonderful, wonderful car, with this pompous bore by my side? Couldn't I get rid of him and his dreary talk, and just enjoy the car, this superb concentration of power that was now fully at my command, responsive to my slightest touch, an infinitely mighty, unconquerable extension of myself? For ever; on like this for ever—ecstasy everlasting, the sudden flash of light going by, the shaft of light ahead, pin-pointing the ever moving end—the end that when it comes is bliss. And then you close your eyes briefly and it is the delirium of movement, of anticipation. And yet you are in control:

not yet, not yet. Draw out the foreplay, the end is not yet. The great moment of breaking relief is not yet.

What is this feeble, babbling voice? Rather fast? Aren't we going rather fast? Well, of course we are, and we're going together, my beauty, my lovely long sleek powerful beauty; but not yet. Let us enjoy each other just a little longer, a little longer, you at my command.

12

He cheated me at the last. I was in my dream of fulfilment and put off the moment for too long. I was weak with longing for the end and he saw his chance. I do not know how he did it, because his arm was injured and helpless. I had counted on that. But he turned the ignition key and then grasped the wheel and the rushing and the speeding grew less and less and we came, slowly, slowly, to a stop. I should have done it then. The slightest twist of my arm could yet have been enough; his left hand held so awkwardly could not have stopped me. But I could not, in cold blood, swing the wheel and bring about the crash that even in my dream of power and completion I had not been able to accomplish. I was nervous, formed of common clay; I did not want to die. I had been cheated of my dream, thrust back from the brink of ecstasy into the heavy awkwardness of common life.

The night was dark; a cool breeze blew round us in the open car. There seemed to be some sort of embankment at the side of the road and a few yards ahead, in the beam of the headlamps, was a square shape like a telephone booth. It reminded me for a fleeting moment of the view from my window.

He got out of the car.

"What's the matter?" I asked. I was still bewildered, disorientated.

"Going to phone the A.A.," he said, "and ask them for a tow."

"But there's nothing the matter with the car. It's running perfectly."

"Perfectly! And I thought you were a driver! Can't you hear the row it's making—the vibration? God knows what's the matter, but I'm not letting you drive it back in this state, thank you. Won't be long."

He walked towards the A.A. box, a tall dark shadow with a blur at the side where the right arm was hanging limply half out of its sling. At first I did not understand. Of course there was nothing wrong with the car, and I could prove it at once. I felt for the ignition. He had taken the key. I saw it at once; of course, he was not going to telephone the A.A. at all; he was going to telephone the police. He was going to hand me over. But what for? I had done nothing. I had offered to drive him home, and then I had said I liked driving the car and could we go on a little please, and he had said yes, and we had gone on. That was all. Except that I had talked. What had I said? I had told him who I was and he had pretended he had not known it before. He had been very stupid and obstinate and the conversation had not gone at all as I had expected. And I was still left with the final burden; that I was sure I had not shared with him.

I began to cry. It was too bad. All this planning, all this terrible anxious waiting, and it ended nowhere. I had got nothing out of it but the pleasure of driving a very fast car for a short while. So what next? I thought of getting out and running, while he was in the A.A. box. If only he had left the key I could have driven away, on and on and on into the night, recapturing my dream, starting all over again in some northern town. Perhaps I should meet another Judy to bring me yet again that little lift of the heart and that hope for what the next day might bring. But to get out and walk, for miles perhaps, along this dark unwelcoming road until I found a train or bus, and then to be looked at, wondered at, to have to explain myself, to be caught up in the straitjacket of tickets and timetables and turnstiles and hotel reception clerks—no, that was something I could not face. I must get home and think up something else. But now I would have to be very, very careful. I had talked too much; I had put him on his guard. He could prove nothing, and the police could prove nothing. But they would watch me; there would be eyes and whispers everywhere.

Headlamps flashed by. The vibration from the heavy lorries shook the car in which I sat. The light and the sound died away and there was just this little island of light and life and security in all the surrounding blackness. I knew I ought to move, but could not. He came back towards the car and I wondered how I could ever have hated and feared him. He was a poor thing; too weak or too stupid to make use of the hold he had had over me. He was wiping his forehead; he seemed to be shaking as if from nerves or from pain. A coward, I thought; bullies so often are.

"They're sending someone from Potter's Bar in about ten minutes," he said, and the voice was pure Nigel Reeves falsetto. "Are you all right? I'm going to find a hedge or a tree—if there is one. Shan't be long."

He disappeared into the darkness behind, and I knew he would not return until he could see the breakdown van approaching. He was afraid of me. How senseless had been my fear of all these weeks! I had completely misunderstood. He had known my story, most of it, and guessed the rest. He had been trying to find out, no doubt, to confirm his fears so that he could worry all the more. He was a poor thing. But frightened things, when cornered, can turn nasty, and I had only a very short time left to make my own escape.

The heavy lorries flashed and shook. I switched off the lights of the sports car. It was very dark. Even if he were only a few yards away he would not see me cross the road.

It was hateful to leave the lovely car. The road was clear and I ran across, paused a moment on the grass between the carriageways, and then went on to the further side. I did not want to be taken back to London just yet, but it was too risky to hail a lorry on the same side of the road as the sports car. It was difficult enough here. They went at such a pace, these monsters. Like express trains, I thought, with the tons and tons of metal that went into their making, and the great loads they were carrying, and their relentless, all-powerful rush through the dark world. Heaven help anyone or anything that got in their way. I had never driven such a vehicle. How I should love to sit at the wheel, have all that power at my finger-tips!

But not just now. I had a very different role to play. At last one stopped, in very good time, not forcing me to jump for my life as had the others. The driver was a youngish chap with a resigned and mournful face and a quiet voice.

I told my story. My mind was working very clearly now, but my state of nerves was such that my voice came out shakily, and it did not take much acting to make my manner appear distraught. It was my boy friend, I said—and I hoped that in the dark, with my hairdo and my make-up and the clothes I wore, I could look like someone who would get into such a fix—it was my boy friend, and he was terribly temperamental and difficult, and I had always been rather scared of him, and we'd been at a party, and he'd got the idea I was talking too much to another man, and when we came away in his car he got more and more crazy and was threatening to crash the car and finish us both . . .

Here I had to pause for my long shuddering gasps of horror, while the lorry-driver said: "Take it easy now," and made soothing and reassuring noises.

"Anyway," I concluded after many swallowings and false starts and dabbings of my eyes, "thank God something went wrong with the car and we had to pull in and he got out to phone the A.A.—and as soon as it looked safe I ran and ran—and here I am, and for God's sake can you get me somewhere away quick—anywhere, wherever you're going!"

It very nearly did not come off. The wretched boy believed me all right, but he had a conscience.

"You get in, ma'am. I'll see you're all right and he doesn't trouble you. But I'd better go and see if I can help him get going first. Which way's his car? Where did you break down?"

I could have screamed. "The other side," I said, "a few hundred yards down the road—round the corner beyond the bridge. But he'll be all right. There's an A.A. box. I saw it. Oh please, *please* take me on! I can't *stand* any more of him tonight—I'm scared stiff. *Please* let's go!"

He wavered a little longer and then climbed back into the driver's seat. "All right. Where d'you live? Where do you want to go?"

"I live in central London—but I don't know if I'd better go home—I'm on my own in the flat. He might turn up there later—he's capable of anything. Oh look here, could we just drive along a little while I think what to do?"

My voice sounded very fearful. He took the hint and said nothing. I sat on my uncomfortable seat, my head bent, crying quietly as I was expected to do, while my mind worked.

Of course Malcolm had not phoned the A.A. He must have phoned the police. That was definite. He would not have expected me to get out and run—he would be surprised to find me gone. But what story had he told? That he knew my identity? Yes, but I had been acquitted after fair trial. Nothing they could do there. That I had tried to kill him from the balcony? No conceivable proof of that—never would or could be any. That I had kidnapped him and was intending to kill us both in his car? Again no proof. He had asked me to drive him home and I had agreed, and he had agreed that we should go on. Nothing criminal there. For all the police knew I had been going to turn at the next roundabout and take him home. It was he who was going to look the fool when they came. They would believe part of his story, of course, because obviously he had not driven out there by himself with a broken shoulder or whatever it was. But how would he explain my disappearance? What would they suspect had really happened? They might conclude that I had run off because I was afraid of him—which a defenceless woman might well be, caught in such a situation late at night miles from anywhere. After all, the lorry driver had believed my story.

But the lorry driver had not known about the injured arm. Oh damn that arm! It had served its purpose; it was nothing but a nuisance now. There must be a very strong motive to induce an able-bodied driver to run away from an injured man in such a place. What could it be? He had threatened me, of course. I wasted several minutes in fruitless wondering how to tell my story, still shrunk in my corner, my face still covered with my handkerchief, until I recollected that I was not yet on trial, was not even being questioned; there was neither need nor opportunity for me to defend myself to anyone. Malcolm would pour out his confused and incredible tale. Even if they believed him, there was nothing they could do. They would tell him to keep his eyes open, to let them know if he had any further suspicions, to bring them evidence if he ever found any.

But would he also tell Judy? Of course he would not, I told myself, because it would mean he had no longer any hold over me; but try as I might to believe this, I could not convince myself, because there seemed to be a flaw in my reasoning somewhere, and I could not trace it. And then suddenly I could think no more, my mind was exhausted and my body was aching and weary and I longed to be out of this noisy, bumping lorry and in quiet comfort alone.

"I think perhaps I'd better go to a hotel," I told the lorry driver in my sobbing voice. "I don't want to bother any friends at this time of night, but I really am scared to go home—he's going to be more mad with me than ever for running away. I suppose there's nowhere you know along here where it would be all right to turn up at this hour?"

He was very doubtful, but after many sighs of weariness on my part he recollected that we were within a few miles of a recently opened motel, just off the main road. I persuaded him to drop me at the corner. I was glad to be alone again. He was a miserable, irritating creature.

I walked slowly along to the entrance of the motel, composing myself, switching over to another personality. I passed through the door with just the right degree of self-confidence. My clothes and my voice were a sure passport. And, of course, my purse. The sleepy receptionist made no objection to entering the booking for my husband and myself and showing me to the cabin.

"He's just as obstinate as most men," I chattered brightly. "He won't send for a breakdown gang and he won't ask for help, and although he says he can fix it in five minutes, I've had all this before, and I don't fancy sitting there the next three hours in the dark while he pokes about inside the bonnet! Anyway, I got a lift to the corner—and he knows where to come, so if you could just give him the number when he turns up—and I'd better pay you now, hadn't I?—and yes, we'll want breakfast. Don't make it too early—heaven knows what time he'll get to bed. Oh yes, our luggage—well I wasn't going to lug the suitcases myself, and in any case I always put a toothbrush in my bag and I'll just have to manage till he comes. I can lie down and get some rest, anyway."

She had not the least suspicion. I signed the register as Mr. and Mrs. Roberts, and I kept my white glove on my ringless left hand.

— 13 —

I have been here nearly a week now. It is not unlike the hospital. A little bare white room overlooking a gravel path and a privet hedge. I can just see the outline through the net curtains as I lie in bed, and I remember the view from my window in the square and grieve that it is not here with me. The cars come and go, and the people slam the doors and call out to each other, but it all passes me by. I feel very peaceful.

It was well worth all that tiresome business with the manager of the motel before I was allowed to stay. I was sick to death of putting on the hysteria, of explaining how I had suspected all along that my husband was going with another woman and wanted to get rid of me, but I never dreamed, till after waiting in vain for him to appear I telephoned home and learnt the truth, that he would do it in such a beastly manner—leaving me high and dry like that after pretending the car had broken down. No, I didn't want to go and stay with friends. I just wanted a bit of peace for a few days. I would have to go to a hotel in any case. Couldn't I stay here? And was there a shop where I could get a few necessary things—including some writing paper, because actually I was an author of sorts, and I thought it might calm me down a little to get on with my work.

Naturally I would pay in advance. Cash, or would they take a cheque?

A cheque would do?—Good, but it would be signed in my other name, the name I wrote under. No, they probably would not have heard of me—it was rather specialist sort of stuff that I wrote. If I could have my meals, and not be disturbed, and if I could make telephone calls when I needed to.

It surprises me that they swallowed it all. I have always known I could act a little, but I must have inherited even more of the art than I thought I had from my parents. So here I am, the mystery woman in number seventeen, and I do not think I can remain more than a day or two longer. But I have done what I wanted to do, and that is, to write the whole story for Judy—the story of my love for her and my sacrifice for her. It is all down now, in three cheap exercise books, in my small and legible writing so that she will have no difficulty in reading it. I feel better for having told her; I think she will understand me now.

But how to get this to her? That I do not yet know. What are you doing at this moment, Judy? Now, as I lie here looking at the late evening sunlight slanting along the privet hedge, thinking of you, what are you doing now? Who is at this moment looking on those liquid eyes, that sweet rosebud softness of your mouth? Do you think of me? Do you remember me? Do you worry what has become of me—wonder where I am, how I am? What has Malcolm told you? Has he made you hate me? You won't hate me when you have read this, I am sure. You will pity me, grieve for the suffering to which your beauty has brought me. Perhaps it will please your vanity that your loveliness should at the beginning have lit me up with hope for the future, as I have tried to show you it did. And you must now pity me, now that all those hopes have gone.

I wonder if I have written something that I ought not to have written. Sometimes I have become confused, living every moment through again as I wrote, and I did not know whether I was talking to you or to Robert or to myself. I am not sure even now. I think perhaps, after all, I have been writing this for Robert. Yes, it must be for Robert because I have told it like a story, picking out the dramatic moments to hold the listener's attention and awaken his curiosity; withholding the climax until the last moment in order to heighten the excitement. I have made an *histoire* of it, and only Robert ever had the patience to listen to my *histoires*. They are terribly boring, really; I hate having to hear other people's. But if one has this little element of melodrama in one's character, then one has to express it somehow.

How I do miss Robert! How could they ever have imagined that it was he whom I wanted to destroy! How can I ever forget the horror, the unbelief, the utter helplessness to prevent it, when I saw, as my foot went down on the brake just the calculated six inches from the edge, that the one whom I had believed to be standing between the back of the car and the water was still standing, momentarily transfixed in horror too, a foot away, and the one in the water below was—was my own dear husband! He had moved, moved from the grasp that had been holding him in safety. Why had he done so? He had never done it before, but had always waited to be guided. Had he known what was in my mind? Had he guessed all and, finding it more than he could bear, taken this as his own way out? Or was it his own subtle revenge? A good chess player looks many, many moves ahead. Had he at that moment seen it all, looked into the future with his sightless eyes and known what it would do to me? Did he hate me so?

I shall never know now. It does not really matter. Nothing matters. I am lost and lonely without my story to write, my view to look at. I have no aim, no hope. Judy's beauty is dimmed. The evil one who is always with her and who has in the end escaped me—he still lives. He has conquered and I have no means of hitting back. I have a large bottle half full of my sleeping pills—enough to send two or three people to everlasting oblivion. I could take them now with the tea that the plump little Italian girl has just brought me. She has a kind face and liquid dark eyes, but her hair is greasy and lank and she looks rather stupid. I shut my eyes and I remember Judy. Estelle—Judy. Which have I loved the more? Judy has been kind, Estelle never. She hated me from the day Robert told her I was going to marry him; she knew the hold she had over me and tortured me. The wretched Derek—of course she cared nothing for him. A tool, that was all. And yet how I suffered! How she would pet him and praise him and hint—and more than hint—at his prowess as a lover! But never when Robert was there, oh no. To him she was always the sweet innocent, and he could not see that her face had changed, that she had grown to look old and used and knowing. And Derek so polite, so respectful to Robert. But how he sneered at me, the dirty little rat! No wonder my hatred rose and rose until it burst. It was more than flesh and blood could stand, what those two did to me.

But where am I? I am wandering. I was going to bring my story to a close. Quietly, here in this unloving and feature-less room with the white terylene curtains already going slightly grey, and the newly painted green woodwork showing the dirty smudges of fingers. Empty, empty. Empty with the transitoriness of the thousands who will pass through; the couples who will wash and undress and sleep and eat their breakfast; who will quarrel, perhaps, over the next day's journey, over the past day's misdeeds; who will exchange a myriad trivial thoughts; who will kiss and who will copulate—an act as meaningless, as lacking in emotion, as cold and bare as the room. Transitory, empty. No mark of human feeling, of love, hope or despair, rests here. The characters of those who slept here on the first night are as dim, as unprojected as are the characters of those who will sleep here on the one-thousandth night and of all those in between. Wash, eat, sleep, dress, go to the lavatory, talk, embrace each other. Of such things do our lives consist. Such is the bare skeleton of human activity. It is nothing unless it is decked out with our own personalities, and our own personalities are nothing if they have not been made by love.

Who will mourn if I die here alone, the mystery woman in number seventeen, whose purse commands acquiescence and false smiles of goodwill? And if I have no mourner, of what avail to die? Only the loved should take their lives; the unloved should not take them, for they take what has no value. If someone would grieve—be it only ever so little— for me, then I could die, and gladly.

The plump Italian will not grieve. She will be excited, she too will have a tale to tell. The manager will not grieve. He will be angry and afraid that such an accident might do harm to his business. My friends that once were? Aunt Laura? Professor Barlow? They will be shocked at first. That much my end will move them. But they will not grieve; they will be freed from a burden—from the burden of feeling that they ought to do something for me. They will be relieved of that nagging relentless knowledge of an-other's misery, that knowledge that casts a shadow over the joys and contentments of the sensitive and conscientious spirit. They will be shocked a little, and then they will be glad.

My eyes are dim. I sit on the edge of the low bed with its nondescript candlewick cover, and tears fall on to the page as I write. It helps to write. The cheap little exercise book is my friend, the only friend I have, the recipient of all my confidences, a kindly, patient hearer. Some great man—was it Goethe?—has said that so long as one can write, one is saved. Perhaps I may yet be saved. But someone must mourn for me; someone must care a little.

I think Judy does care. I believe that my going will leave

a little gap in her life. But only so long as her mind has not been poisoned against me.

I have delayed too long. While I have lain here, Malcolm has had his chance. He will have told her all. But will she believe him? Will she not say: You are accusing her and she is not here to defend herself—wait, wait and see what she has to say. Have I yet a chance? Oh Judy, if you will but hear me! You shall pity me! Heavens, you shall pity me! "Oh you shall not rest between the elements of earth and air but you shall pity me." *Twelfth Night,* isn't it? That was one of my mother's greatest roles—Viola.

But I wander again. I must find out. Does Judy know? I must return to the house in the square, once more creep in unseen. I have a plan. The partition between our rooms is very thin. In the corner where my bed stands, the corner where I always hear the most of what goes on next door, there is some paper peeling away about four feet up from the floor. I notice it when I lie in bed. If I pull it away further, and scrape off some of the nasty mess of paint and paper that lies beneath the top layer, and if I hold my ear close to the flimsy wood underneath, then I should be able to hear much of what they say. They will not bother to lower their voices, as they sometimes do, since they will not expect me to be there. And when I have learned how much they know, why then I shall once more know what to do. So I will pack up my things, pay my final bill here, and then back to Bloomsbury, plotting all the while how I can get into the house without being seen.

How good it is to plot and act again!

14

It is taking a terrible risk, to write in my exercise book like this, but I find I cannot now do without it. Only by confiding my *histoire* to these cheap ruled pages can I soothe my overstrung nerves; only by confining my bold ingenious schemes within the limits imposed by grammar and punctuation, there to be critically studied and reviewed, can I judge whether they will in fact succeed. I will find some way to destroy these books; perhaps it will not be necessary. I do not know how it will turn out, but I know I must keep up my courage and not lose my head. And so I must write.

It was a difficult problem, getting back unseen into the house. The evenings are long and light and mild, and people are about late in the streets. There was no sense in waiting till evening. Since it had to be done in daylight, it was best done in the dead hours of the afternoon. I got a taxi to fetch me from the motel and take me to Potter's Bar, and then I came by bus and tube to Great Russell Street. That was simple enough. Now came the great decision: should I try at the front door or at the back? The risk of being seen was far greater at the front, but once inside, there was only the one staircase up to my room. It all depended on the caretaker's wife. The man worked as a porter and would certainly not be there. But what would an eight months pregnant woman in that position be doing at three-thirty on a weekday afternoon? I decided to approach the square from the other side, keeping close in under the high and bushy shrubs along the gravel walks, while I debated what to do.

She might be out shopping, but more likely she would be resting. Where? Not in a deckchair alongside those filthy dustbins, surely. The kitchen was at the back of the basement flat, and Mrs. Willows had had her bed in the stuffy front room where she received the rents. They might have changed all that, though, and they might even lock the back door. I could not count on the incredible casualness of Mrs. Willows's days. Poor old wretch. She must have felt too miserable even to be frightened. For a moment my mind strayed from the job in hand, and I wondered what had become of her. She would have let me in; I should have had no problem there.

A turn in the path brought me opposite the house, and I paused to look at it. All the dirty paint, the broken ironwork, the assortment of shabby curtains at the windows, could not destroy its perfect proportions nor entirely dim its elegance. It made me feel sad and nostalgic. There was not a sign of life anywhere, and I was beginning to think that it would be best to take the risk and make a dash for it across the street, when a head of metallic blonde hair appeared above the area railings, and then came a short coat of brilliant scarlet, totally inadequate cover for the swollen figure beneath. I retreated hastily behind a lilac bush, and then my heart began to thump and my breath came short, because she was coming straight towards me, across the roadway and into the square.

It was a trap. She had seen me. She would come close up to me and say: This is the one! And then police would emerge from the bushes, from every corner of the square.

For a moment I was held motionless in panic, and then a couple of young mothers strolling along with their prams gave me a casual glance, and I found the strength to glance back and to walk unconcernedly along. I was losing my head again; of course she had not seen me, and if I kept quietly along the path I could escape from the gardens without being noticed. Even better, I knew now that she was out of the house and there was a good chance that I could get in through the back door. Fifty-fifty, anyway, that it was not locked. Women of her sort are often careless about everything except their own appearance. They dress themselves up to the nines to go out, but leave mess and muddle behind them. Besides, she had no shopping bag, and it looked very probable that she was only going to sit in the gardens. The better to keep watch on the house, maybe.

I came safely out into the side street, walking briskly and looking back once or twice to make sure that the caretaker's wife was still out of my sight, behind the bushes, and gained the entrance to the builder's yard without attracting any attention. The same assortment of junk lay in the same positions as before, and there was no one about. I pushed open the door in the wall and the stink of the dustbins rose up at me. Nothing was altered. Now came a bad moment: crossing the yard. No sense in hesitating, just get it over quick, it's your only chance.

It was done. It took about forty seconds from the time of coming round the dustbins to the moment of sitting panting on my bed. The back door was open and there was not a sign of life on either flight of stairs. After all, it was not so very surprising, during the quietest part of the afternoon, that there should be a period of forty seconds with nobody about. It would not be surprising if there should be such a period of forty minutes. They could not watch round the clock and it would never occur to them that I would get in the back way. The neat and elegant Miss Wentworth among the flies and the filth of the refuse dump!

For a moment I sat smiling in triumph, and then it seemed to me cruel that I should have to creep in to my own home like this, and I felt anger once again. I got up to see whether anything had been tampered with, and on the little table I found a piece of cheap paper with a few words scrawled in an illiterate hand: "Miss Wentworth—come and see me when you get back. Caretaker."

What presumption! Wretched young man! No "please" about it. How dared he? But of course, I realised when my initial indignation had subsided a little, I owe a week's rent, that is all. Well, it would have to wait. Whether or not I would reveal myself would depend entirely on what I heard this evening. I was about to crumple up the note when some deep instinct told me: No, leave it where it was; leave everything just as it was. So I noted carefully the exact positions of the chairs and the way the cushions on the bed were propped up against the wall and other details, and then I put away in drawers the few things I had bought for use at the motel, taking care to leave the top of the drawer looking just as it had done before. And then I made tea and ate the ham sandwich that I had bought in the snack bar near the tube station. I enjoyed it thoroughly. It was delightful to sit once more looking out at my view. At five o'clock I listened carefully to make sure the coast was clear, and then I ran down to the bathroom.

After that I settled myself for the evening's siege. I was amazed how calm I was. I shifted the cushions, laid a sheet of newspaper on the bed to catch the dust, and scraped away at the paper. It came off easily and I had the great good luck to find a knot in the wood underneath so that, working very carefully with a sharp knife, I was even able to prise some of the wood away. All this was achieved before anyone came home from work. How useful is my practical ability now! You fancy yourself as a handyman, Tom Prescott, but in resource and ingenuity you are a babe as compared with myself. But of course it is often very convenient to keep quiet about one's gifts. I settled myself comfortably on the bed with my ear to the wall. My only regret was that I dared not light a cigarette.

I was not the least bit impatient. I was enthralled, rather, to hear Judy come in, throw down her handbag—for that I guessed must be the little thud—and then give a great long-drawn-out sigh. Then it sounded as if she was kicking something across the room—whatever could that be?—and then there was a creak of springs that told me she had flopped down into the oldest and most comfortable armchair; and then there was another long sigh, and yet another, and a sort of whining muttering sound that could have been "I dun-no."

How extraordinary, I thought quite dispassionately; does she know she is doing it? Do any of us know the curious movements and sounds we make when we believe ourselves to be unheard and unobserved? Probably not; and yet our social inhibiting mechanism is so strong and automatic that we would never make them had we the least suspicion that another ear or eye could hear or see.

Judy got up soon afterwards, and moved noisily about the room, left the door open when she went down to the bathroom, banged it loudly on her return, and then there were intervals of silence when she had presumably gone into their little room at the back. Intermittently I heard the heavy sighing and the muttering. What's the matter with the girl, I thought irritably; has she got a pain or something?

Then Tom came in. Now I should hear something, and all that sighing business would stop, thank heaven. Judy spoke:

"Hullo, darling. I got sausages again. I hope you don't mind."

Fantastic. Had I not known how beautiful they looked, those lips from which these earth-shaking words were uttered, what a miserable little wretch would I have imagined the speaker to be! For the first time I began to regret my action. Could I really endure it, listening to this sort of thing for the next few hours? Perhaps they would not even mention me. Perhaps Malcolm would not come. Perhaps they had quarrelled at last; perhaps he was ill in bed. Perhaps anything. Oh, on what a mountain of assumptions had I rested all my hopes!

For the next half hour, while a meaningless recital of who had said what to whom in the office today went on next door, I lay doubting and fearing. And then a remark of Tom's brought my courage back.

"Are these all the biscuits we've got? Haven't we got anything better to offer Malcolm?"

Thank God! He *was* coming, then.

A silly little wrangle followed, and then, as they were eating, Judy said: "You really do like the flat, don't you, Tom? I mean—if you'd rather wait and see some others first I could stick it here a bit longer." She sounded very plaintive.

"Why? Don't *you* like it?"

"Yes, of course, darling, it's super. But it's an awful lot of money."

"Oh do stop worrying about that, Judy. We've been over it already. You've got to get out of here quick or you'll have a nervous breakdown. That's flat."

"But we might find something cheaper." A little nagging whine. Poor Tom, I thought, he will get to know this very well, and hate it more and more, in the years to come.

"We might, but I doubt it. It's more important for you to keep well and keep on with your job. It's only a fifteen year mortgage and we'll be able to pay Malcolm back by the end of three years with luck."

Aha! So that was it, was it? A nice posh flat paid for with Malcolm's money. I wondered when they were moving. I should have to act very fast, perhaps, I listened carefully, and gathered that it was to be in two weeks' time. The flat appeared to be in Hampstead. Next door to our noble benefactor, no doubt, I thought, where he can keep his eye on them. And then for a moment the protective glaze of

indifference which had mercifully surrounded me since I
began my vigil wore a little thin, and the demon jealousy
intruded once again. She will owe it to him! And it was
I who was to furnish her with her dream home!

But I hastily controlled myself, because this was much
too important to allow emotion to cloud my perceptions.
They talked then a great deal about the flat. It seemed to me
that Tom was making a deliberate effort to keep Judy's mind
on it. It became very boring after a while, and I believe I
dozed a little against my pillows.

I came to with a start to hear someone rattling at my door.

"Is anyone there?"

I cowered in my corner, my heart and lungs bursting.

"Is anyone there?"

Another rattle, and then a silence, and I knew that he was
standing close up against the flimsy door, his ear to the
crack, listening, sensing whether the room was empty or
not.

My God, what shall I do, what shall I do! Will he break
it down? Will he go to the caretaker and fetch the master
key? Oh help me, help me now!

My prayer was answered. Tom's voice spoke, outside my
door: "She's not there, Malcolm. I checked with the
Burtons before I came up."

"You're quite sure? She couldn't have got in without
them seeing?"

"No. It's quite impossible. Mrs. Burton went up to check
at about tea-time, and after that she was cleaning windows
and keeping a good lookout till Judy came in."

I clutched my throat and thanked God for that lazy, lying,
pregnant woman downstairs.

"All the same—I'd like to make sure."

I held my breath again.

Then Judy's voice: "Oh Malcolm, do come in—honestly
there's no one there. I've not heard a soul. I feel so awful,

being such a nuisance to everyone like this. Do come in, the coffee's getting cold."

They moved away. I breathed again. So Judy was frightened of me; hence the sighs, the feared breakdown, the moving to a new luxury flat on Malcolm's money. I knew it all. There was scarcely need to listen further. Of course he had told her everything. He had taken her away from me for ever. And I had let him live. He had been at my mercy, this beast, this foul and evil creature with his puffed-up vanity, this parasite, this monster of which the world ought to be rid. And I had let him go. Mad I had been to let him go.

For a while I gave way to despair. Silent, unweeping, unsobbing; always aware that not the least sound must issue from my room. And then, as I lay with my ear to the wall, barely hearing now the voices next door, inspiration came to me. Had I not yet a chance? The hole in the partition. My sole means of contact. At first I thought of fire. How easily could I set their room alight! But of course it would not do. It would be instantly discovered and extinguished if they were there; and if they were not there, to what avail? And in either case I would myself be instantly smoked out and lost.

But they have nothing on you, I told myself. There is only suspicion still, no proof, no proof. How do I know they aren't setting a trap, was my next thought. A trap to snare me into confession. No. I dared not risk it. At all costs I must not be seen. I had but one weapon left, that they did not know I was there. And I was safe only for tonight. Tomorrow, no doubt, that fecund slattern would be coming up with her master key.

The weak spot in the wall. There must be a way. I looked out at my view. It was bright in the late evening sunshine. There was as yet no glimpse of pink or yellow in the sky. Then my eyes turned around the room and I saw it. Of course. The gas. That shaky old portable fire with the long flexible tubing. But it still would not reach. It would need more tubing to bring it across. Oh, how I could have wept, but dared not make a sound!

It is dark now, and I write by the light of the streetlamp as I sit at my window. There are no bright colours in the view, just the dark outlines against the eternally pink glow of the London sky. I would like to sit like this for ever. Could time but stop; could I but end peacefully, quietly, unknowing. Could some unseen hand switch on the gas behind me. I would not resist; I would sit patiently waiting. But I cannot do it myself. I cannot. And my time is very short. I have only tonight.

My little book, my only friend. I do not know how I shall find the courage. The risks I have to take! I must steal out at dead of night, conceal myself till morning; buy the tubing and other needs, and then creep back in the afternoon as I did today. And even then it is a thousand to one against success. The smell of gas—they will know at once. But even here my luck still holds, because they have been spraying their little bits of furniture—the old cupboard by the door and the bookcase by the window—with woodworm-killer. I heard them say so. They do not want to risk taking woodworm into their nice new flat. And it smells terribly strong; I noticed it when I came in. It will disguise for a while the smell of gas. But until they are too weak to act? Ah, dare I hope so? But I must not think. I have no other way. If all else fails I shall have my knife. Not the little sharp one I used this afternoon; but the big one that I am going to buy. And now, my tired brain, to work. Where to go? The stories to tell the shop-keepers. How to fix the tube, how to make the hole. Oh, how lucky that the cushion covers the patch, that I did not destroy the caretaker's note, that I had the forethought to leave all in the room exactly as it was! The house has a thousand eyes. They see me, every one.

* * *

It has succeeded so far. It was not too difficult to get out.
They always leave the front door on the Yale lock alone. I
did not slam it, but closed it softly with my own key. It was
miserable, in the waiting-room at the station; it was like a
dead world. I had a few curious glances directed at me, but
I did not have to tell any story. That remained for the
hardware shops. Oh, what rubbish I had to relate, and how
bored I was with it! Bored, bored, bored. But I got all I
required in the end. And later on I rested quite comfortably
in the waiting-room of the other big terminus, and now I am
safely back, in spite of the caretaker's wife. They are
deceived in her, the lazy slut. I don't believe she has been
up to my room at all today. I could tell them a thing or two.
Or perhaps the baby has started and she is away. It does not
matter. I am here.

It is hard to be patient. I have no hope now that the gas
will succeed. I must have been out of my mind to imagine
that it would. But I have worked so hard, and I have done
such a neat job of fixing the tubing to the socket of the
portable fire and of making the hole in the wall, which is
just behind the cupboard by their door, that I am very loth
to give up the plan. It has cost me too much. I must try it at
least. If, by a miracle, it succeeds, then freedom once again
is mine. But if not, then I always have my knife.

How tired I am! I have slept a little and now it is late and
I hear them next door. I believe Malcolm has come. He did
not rattle my door tonight; that will come later, perhaps.
They are talking about the woodworm. What does Judy
say?

"I'm awfully sorry—it's foul, isn't it? It's taking ages to
wear off. But I've had the window open. I had to shut it
because it's a bit breezy. I've got some spray stuff, though.
Wait a moment."

And then Malcolm. "Lavender, they call it? My God, it

smells worse than the other! Do stop it, Judy. You'll asphyxiate us all."

There. I have done it. The gas will soon be pouring through. Behind the cupboard. It is so easy when you are clever that way. How Robert used to admire me! Oh Robert, if you were only here! I write and write, and I am talking to you still.

They have suspected. Malcolm, of course. But Tom says: "I can't smell gas. Can you, Judy?"

"I don't know. I don't think so." Her voice is a plaintive whine.

They move about the room, testing the fire, their cooking-stove, the water-heater. The radio with its endless stream of background noise drowns all along the little sound of the hiss.

"Shall we phone the Gas Board?"

There is a little argument about this. And then suddenly Judy is weeping, and they are both very busy consoling her. What next? My little book, my only comfort now, what next?

Judy speaks. I start; her tearful voice is very very near to where I lie. ". . . a cigarette . . . match, Tom."

NO! Judy, NO, NO, NO!

Extract from letter from John Davies, barrister and amateur viola-player, in reply to a letter from his friend Albert Malcolm Jenkinson:

". . . So that's the Warmouth case as I saw it at the time, and my view has been only too unhappily borne out by subsequent events. It is a pity that you did not ask me about this before, though I confess I do not see how you could possibly have had any suspicions that she was not exactly what she appeared to be. Even the police took the balcony incident at its face value. And after all, heaven forbid, for the sake of British justice, that we should go about snooping on people who have been acquitted, and following up their every movement. No, I do not think you have been in any way remiss. You did quite right to report it after her 'confession', but after that it was up to the authorities.

"You did all you could in watching out for her possible return. You were getting the Prescotts out of there as soon as you humanly could. Like so many criminal lunatics, she had extraordinary reserves of cunning and daring and, unfortunately also like so many of them, a very great deal of luck. The end was bad enough, but it might have been infinitely worse had it not been for you. How you managed to hold her down after the explosion, and get that knife away, take charge of everything until the police arrived, with your arm like that, and Tom Prescott totally out of control over his wife, and with only the more hysterical members of the household at home and available—well, frankly I shall never know. I am glad that your own injuries were no more severe, but sorry that it has inevitably put back the date of your own recovery. I'm afraid it will be some time yet before we can have another musical evening.

"I hardly know what to say concerning Mrs. Prescott. It is the sort of tragedy that cuts very deep. Surely your friendship and generosity must now be of greater value than ever to them both. You feel that it was your presence that led Mrs. Prescott into such danger and that you are therefore responsible. Could you not equally argue, if you *must* seek an analogy with the Warmouth affair, that it was your presence that saved her? It was, after all, the girl who was the intended victim in that case, for no other reason than imagined rebuffs. Bringing in a boy friend in a desperate attempt to protect herself against her stepmother, she laid herself wide open to the attack. Whereas in this case—except at the very last—you have drawn all danger on to yourself.

"But I am indeed more grieved than I can say about Mrs. Prescott. It is of course a very great relief that at any rate the sight of one eye has been saved; and plastic surgery, as we all know, can work miracles nowadays. She does not lack courage, and she will pull through. Surely in the end she will feel able once more to face other people and to live a normal life. She has her husband, she has her devoted friends, she will have her children. I do beg you to try not to dwell too much on your own share in it.

"You ask financial compensation for victims of criminal attack. Well, in a case like this where the assailant has been committed during Her Majesty's pleasure . . ."